After the
Moon Rises

By

Karilyn Bentley

After the Moon Rises

Cover Art by *RJ Morris*

The Wild Rose Press
PO Box 708
Adams Basin, NY 14410-0706
Visit us at www.thewildrosepress.com

Publishing History
First Black Rose Edition, 2013
Print ISBN 978-1-62830-210-3
Digital ISBN 978-1-62830-211-0

Published in the United States of America

Praise for Karilyn Bentley's *MAGICAL LOVER*

"*MAGICAL LOVER* sweeps you away to a rich fantasy world filled with magic, mystery, and unforgettable characters."

~Trinity Blake

~*~

"I didn't want the story to end. It's a magical blend of romance and fantasy!"

~Angela Hicks

~*~

"Sexy and spellbinding!

~Christie Gibson

~*~

"Ms. Bentley's characters are strong and will defend to the death those they love."

~Aloe, Long and Short Reviews

Werewolves
in
London

by

Karilyn Bentley

Dedication

To my wonderful, supportive hubby, I love you.
And to the Spanksters,
I couldn't have done it without you!

Chapter 1

"Your dog doesn't respect you." Vonda reached down to scratch behind Sam's ear. "I can help you with that problem, but I can't help train him to herd. Do we have a deal?"

Tom took off his hat, scratched his head and slammed it back on as if to hold in steam. Judging from the color of his face, he should have let his hair wave free in the breeze. It might cool things off. One long finger pointed at Sam. One nicely shaped, work hardened finger. The list of things that finger could do to her body rushed through Vonda's brain on fast forward. It didn't help that the man whose finger provoked such lascivious thoughts was the best-looking thing in this little Podunk town.

Why was she thinking such thoughts? *Concentrate, Vonda, concentrate!* Last time she thought this way about a man she was in heat. Oh shit. *Not again.* No wonder Sam stuck to her like proverbial glue.

Wait. Tom's mouth was moving. "...me?"

"Huh? I'm sorry, what did you say?" *Good job Vonda, way to look stupid on your first visit with a client.*

"I said, how can that dog not respect me?"

"Well, dogs see things differently than humans. If you don't act like the alpha, then they assume they are the alpha. That's what creates problems. That's where I can help."

"Yes, yes. I know. But I have other herding dogs. None of them give me problems. What's up with that?" His frustrated green stare bored into her.

Men frustrated so easily. Humans in general. Ever see a canine with hypertension?

Sam licked her hand. She took in a shallow breath when his tongue rasped against her skin and it was then she smelled it. The scent of a man. Not just any man. A man she wanted to mate with. A man about six four, with sandy blond, almost brown hair and green eyes. A man who stood less than three feet from her.

Damn hormones.

If she didn't get out of here soon she'd lose any chance of ever being a dog trainer.

She looked at her wrist. *Two hairs past a freckle.* "Well, all dogs are different and therefore react differently. Look, I really have to run. Do you want me to come back and help you with Sam or not?"

Say yes, say yes, say yes. He opened his mouth, closed it, looked at Sam, then her, then Sam. He sighed. Oh yeah, she had the job.

"Okay. When do you want to start?"

She looked at the evening sky, the oranges and pinks blushing across the horizon. Tonight was one day from the full moon and she felt the pull of its magic creep under her skin, touching the beast inside her, coaxing it out of hiding. She would be hard-pressed not to change for the next three days. Well, Tom had waited this long for help, what would be three more days?

"Thursday. Will that work for you?"

He stuck out his hand. "Sounds good. What time did you want to come out?"

She gripped his hand, holding tight despite the tingles shooting straight into her core from where their palms met. Desire ripped through her hormone sensitive veins and she fought the urge to pull him against her. *Damn heat.* He pulled away, shaking his hand.

"Did you feel that?"

"I'm sorry. Sometimes I build up electricity. Would nine in the morning be okay?"

"Umm, sure."

"Great. Gotta run. It's been real nice meeting you." One last pat to Sam's head and she zipped back to her car.

Thank God she had irregular heat cycles. The last time the heat ran through her veins seemed mild compared to the desire Tom evoked in her, and yet she hadn't resisted the urge to mate. Look how that ended, with her husband screaming to the divorce judge that she was a furry dog.

What had she been thinking? Her ex couldn't even tell the difference between a dog and a wolf.

But he had taught her an important lesson and that was to stay away from men. Electronic devices worked quite well, thank you very much. And until she met Tom McGowan her philosophy had worked. A bit lonely at times—*okay, who was she fooling, all the time*—but a little sacrifice never hurt anyone. Her core tingled as she remembered the electrical spark from his touch, the desire she fought while in his presence. Tom had the potential to shatter her philosophy and her heart. Fear colored her thoughts and made tonight's impending change seem easy in comparison.

****

Tom took a deep breath and held it, trying to get

his bodily functions under control. Anger and arousal, what a combination. At least he'd learned one thing from the shapely brunette, and it wasn't a lack of respect from his newest dog. His hand reached for his crotch, feeling the hard ridge of his arousal. Nice to know the thing still worked.

He'd all but given up on his ability to function as a man since Anita's passing four years ago. And not only did his dick suddenly come on line, but what was up with that electric tingle Vonda gave him when she grasped his hand? Last time he'd felt anything remotely like that was from his mother, and Mom sure hadn't provoked what was going on in his pants.

Maybe he should ask Vonda out. Provided he remembered what to do with a woman on a date. Okay, some parts he remembered quite clearly, which is why he hadn't dated since Anita. How would he explain to the poor woman his lack of arousal? *Really, honey, it's not you, it's me.* Yeah, right. Thinking about how that conversation would go scared him away from the dating scene. Now that things seemed to be working again, he might just give it a try.

Thinking about Vonda drove away the anger he felt over her assessment of Sam and the dog's lack of respect for him. Everyone knew dogs thought of Tom as their natural leader. Sam was just crazy. Who cared what her assessment of the situation was, Tom would take the eye candy any way he could get it.

Dark brown hair, shot with silver highlights, hung to her shoulders and framed an elfin face with amber eyes. She barely reached his shoulder and yet her body moved with the grace of an athlete. He'd love to strip off her clothes and see the play of muscles under her skin as her legs gripped his waist while he...

Tom shook his head, clearing away most of the fantasy. Later tonight he'd marvel he actually managed a fantasy, but for now his ranch deserved his attention, not the woman.

"Come, Sam." Tom patted his leg.

Tongue lolling from the side of his mouth, Sam's ears perked up as he stared intently at Tom's leg. The tongue slipped behind teeth as he stood and shook himself, trotting over to where Vonda's car had been parked.

No respect. Man, that burned.

Tom sighed. As impossible as it seemed, Vonda had a point. "Come on, Layla. Let's go make a round."

Layla rose from where she lay, her arthritic legs shaking as she stood. Her tail wagged like a pendulum as she limped to Tom, who slowed his pace so she walked beside him. At least she respected him.

Sam sat in the driveway staring forlornly after the trail of dust from Vonda's car. Tom felt the instant the dog's attention turned to him as Tom and Layla walked toward Tom's truck. Not one to be left behind, Sam yelped as he ran after them, pole vaulting over Layla so he could lead what he considered his pack to the truck.

His pack, Tom's left ass cheek. Sam had a dominance issue, and Tom had too soft of a heart where canines were concerned. Dogs loved him, recognizing a friendly leader when they saw one. Until Sam came into his life, Tom had great success training dogs.

Sam was a breed unto himself and Tom had no idea what to do with him.

If Tom told him to sit, he walked off, come happened only occasionally and down was more elusive than a willing steer at branding time. No wonder Tom's friend Steve had a friend of a friend more than willing to get rid of Sam.

Tom should get rid of him too, but every time he thought it, the damn dog would lick his hand, staring out of those eyes mismatched blue and brown, and Tom couldn't do it. Sam stayed.

Funny thing was, the dog seemed to like Vonda and Sam didn't give his attentions easily. As far as Tom could see, Sam only liked him and his daughter Elizabeth. Until the sexy dog trainer stepped out of her red SUV, revealing jean-clad legs.

Tom shook his head at the image that thought formed and picked up Layla to put her in the bed of his truck. Sam jumped in without being asked. Tom slammed the tailgate shut and started for the door.

He didn't have much time left before the remaining rays of sunlight slid behind the horizon. Gunning the engine, he started across his property, heading to the last hole the vandals had torn in his fence. They were getting braver; this spot was close to the house, almost within visual distance.

So far the only evidence of the vandals' activities was cut fences. His herd hadn't been touched. The damage wasn't even that extensive, nothing was stolen, so why were they bothering?

The whole thing gave him a bad feeling. As if someone hunted him. Once he arrived at the damaged fence, he hopped out, leaving the dogs in the bed. Correction, Layla stayed in the back of the truck like a good girl. Sam saw the need to jump out and chase a rabbit.

It was useless to call him back. Tom grabbed his

tools and used the remaining sunlight to repair the hole in the barbed wire. He heard Sam barking in the distance, Layla whimpering in reply. The wire felt warm under his palm, through the leather glove. Perhaps his skills honed as a lad and unused since that time still worked. Tom closed his eyes, focusing on the heat, imagining who held the wire before him.

It took a minute before the picture came to him, flashing in fast forward like a racecar, the colors a blur. Concentrating, he brought the whirling pictures into focus, slowing them down until he could make sense of them.

Scents came first, the acid smell of fear, terror, and the sharp tang of blood. The wire dropped from his hand as he stumbled backward, his chest constricting, a tight belt suffocating him. He looked to the house, not seeing the structure, but seeing the light from it glowing on the horizon. A cold finger of darkness swept down his back as he saw in his mind's eye Elizabeth running through the house, playing as ten-year-old girls were wont to do. Alone.

Oh, God, no. Not Elizabeth.

Chapter 2

Vonda slammed the car door and scurried up the steps to her house. Not much time left before the sun slid below the horizon and she needed to be in place when darkness hit. The moon wouldn't rise until complete dark, but the change would happen promptly at sundown. All those rumors about werewolves changing when the full moon rose were a little off. Or at least they were off for her; she knew no other werewolves.

Orphaned when she was two and raised by a foster family in Dallas, Vonda never knew about the wolf within her until puberty came and the change hit. The terror she felt that first time still haunted her. When most girls her age got cramps with their periods, she changed into a beast. Like she could discuss that one with her foster mom. Luckily that first time she didn't share a bedroom and no one saw her. For three days around the full moon she changed into a wolf at sundown and back at sunrise.

After that first time, she learned how to sneak out of the house and stay in the shadows. Winter was the worst, when the nights were long and darkness hit around five thirty. Lying became second nature, fear always present. When she turned eighteen and rented her own place, things became easier. She learned how to hunt, how to temper her amazing physical strength and what the auras around people meant.

Just when she thought she had it all figured out, that being a werewolf was no different than having some strange disease, she went into heat.

Intense sexual urges she couldn't resist accompanied the heat cycle. Any man in her vicinity risked being used like a stud. Not that most men minded. Her ex sure didn't. She, on the other hand, hated how she acted, hated having to get laid like an addict needed to shoot up. While her ex loved her carefree sexual attitude, her conservative upbringing caused her to hate it. But with the heat coursing through her veins, forcing her mind on only one thing, she had no choice; she needed a man like an addict needed a fix. After a whirlwind romance consisting of a bunch of now-embarrassing sex, her ex had proposed, clearly confusing lust with love. Try as she might, she couldn't blame him for using her, not when she returned the favor ten times over.

It lasted all of two months, until her husband saw her change. No amount of great sex could hurdle that barrier. He ran out of their apartment faster than she could howl, screaming Vonda was a dog. How insulting.

And now she was in heat again.

All she could think of was Tom, his scent, the electric zing that shot through her body when his hand touched hers. If she remembered correctly, the heat only lasted the time of the full moon. All she had to do was avoid all men, including Tom, and she shouldn't have a problem.

Vonda dropped her purse on the table by the door, striding down the hall to her bedroom. The house was silent except for the ticking of the mantel clock. Tick, tock, each click of the minute hand tugging her one step closer to the change. Kicking off her shoes, she pulled her T-shirt over her head, laying it on the bed. The bra came next, and she tugged off her jeans, folding them in a neat pile on top of the rest of her clothes. The lace thong made a nice bow on the pile.

She felt the magic now, humming in her veins, flowing along her skin. Not much time remained.

Vonda walked down the hall, into the kitchen and out the back door. Under her feet the grass felt warm, soothing. She stood facing west, watching the sun slip beneath the horizon, drawing its rays across the ground like a web. Magic seeped under her skin, rippling muscles, quickening her heart rate. The power built, until her jaw clenched against the pain. Bones snapped, elongating, shortening, changing. Fur streamed over her skin as her hands turned into paws.

Dropping to the ground on all fours, the wolf let loose a howl, shaking the pain free. The grass sprang under her feet as she padded toward the edge of her property.

The hunt was on.

As a wolf, she followed her instincts. As a human, she followed reason. Despite her upbringing, or lack thereof, she learned how to merge her wolf's mind with her human one; how to use her heightened senses no matter what physical state she was in. She listened to her instincts now. They were never wrong when it came to food and that meant food ran ten miles to the east.

A good night's exercise.

Howls sounded from the direction she headed. Her heart leapt at the sound. Cousins. Not a hundred percent like her, but close enough. Wolves accepted her into their packs, although they remained wary of her, uncertain if she was an alpha or omega. Vonda never fought for status in a pack, why should she—even though they were cousins, she didn't belong with them.

She didn't fit in anywhere. As a human she was stronger, faster and had a big hairy secret. As a wolf, her scent smelled like a human, puzzling her cousins, causing them to remain wary of her. She walked among both worlds but belonged to neither.

But at least here in London, Montana she could become a wolf without worrying if humans saw her furry half. There were no wild wolves in Dallas or anywhere in Texas that she knew of. Moving to Montana had been self-preservation and so far, it had been a good move.

No one questioned one extra wolf roaming here and she didn't have to hide for three days like she used to. Why she waited so long to move here was beyond her. She should have moved sooner.

Maybe then she could have avoided the ex. She could have had Tom instead.

Stop it, Vonda! Tom needed to be avoided. At least until the heat went away. Thank God her next appointment with him was after the full moon. Hopefully the heat would be gone then too.

Howls sounded to her right and she veered toward them. She saw images in her mind, images sent by her cousins, their way of communicating. A herd of deer standing in a copse of trees, their ears pricking forward, listening. Feelings of quietness, the hush of paws on grass, the excitement of the impending kill crept through her veins.

Telepathy rocked.

Vonda found her cousins watching the deer, biding their time. She trotted to the back of the hunting party and lowered her tail and ears. The wolves nearest to her sniffed her in a proper how-do-you-do. She felt their uncertainty, but they didn't chase her off and more images of wolves killing deer slashed through her mind.

And then they were running, the deer sprinting away, wolves pounding after them.

Vonda stayed in the back, helping chase, but not taking down a deer. She wouldn't eat first either, that treat belonged to the alpha pair.

Trees flashed by her as she sprinted after the deer, low foliage slapping her face. The smells of the forest excited her, the word "home" a constant thought. Her breath sawed in and out of her lungs, she really needed to hit the track in human form.

Three feet from the deer, she smelled *them* on the evening breeze. A scent that left her salivating. *Cattle*. Directly to her left.

She veered. To hell with the deer. Why have venison when she could dine on steak tartare?

Even as a human she liked her meat raw. And what better to eat than steak, straight off the steer?

Vonda thought the image of cattle and sent it to the nearest wolf who stumbled in his flight after his dinner. Emotions crashed over her, fear, fright, followed by thoughts of humans. Bad, scary, she should stay where it's safe, where humans with explosive sticks couldn't hurt her.

She almost stopped, but why should she be scared of the humans? She was half human after all. And there was steak, did she mention that? Raw, fresh. Much better tasting than deer.

Adios cousins, she was on a new chase.

Her legs picked up speed, churning dirt and leaves as she raced across the ground. A barbed wire fence stopped her progress. The cattle lowed on the other side.

Close. So close. She could dine on steak tartare tonight. Her stomach growled.

Vonda eyed the fence. Two rows of barbed wire were strung between wooden posts. It didn't look like an electrical fence. The fence was meant to keep animals in, not out. And as a werewolf she had her own way of getting through the fence that her canine brethren found impossible to do.

She ducked her head between the two wires, following with her left front leg, then left rear leg. The right side followed and she was through. The cattle looked her way. She snarled and leapt.

Cattle scattered as the wolf attacked. Not as fast as deer, they still ran for their lives. Vonda picked out one at the back of the pack and jumped at its throat, taking it down. The cow screamed, the sound ending in a gurgle as its throat tore open, blood streaming. She shook her head, spraying blood across the grass.

She waited until the blood slowed to a trickle, the spirit of the cow flying free. Once it was dead, Vonda sank her teeth into its hide. *Dinner, ah.*

Steak tartare never tasted so good. Her monthly treat since she arrived in town three months ago. Last thing needed was for wolves to be blamed for monthly cattle killing, which is why she tried to hit a different ranch each month. Problem was she hadn't learned the boundary lines of each rancher or who all the ranchers were. Tom was the only one she'd met and he managed to turn her on even when she was in wolf form.

From the darkness came barking, riding the wind as it blew across the ground. She raised her blood-soaked muzzle and inhaled the wind. A dog was closing in, running full force toward her. Shouldn't be a problem, dogs lacked the strength of wolves.

You can't be seriously considering killing a dog, Vonda. Get real! Her human mind overrode the wolf's instincts and she turned and faced the oncoming dog.

Vonda snarled at it, baring teeth, letting it know the cow belonged to her. A brown and white dog pulled up short, its tail initially dropping, then curling as it snarled back.

Tom wasn't kidding around when he said Sam presented a problem. The damn dog was willing to go up against a wolf, and a werewolf at that. Not the smartest animal around, but Vonda had to give him points for bravery. Or maybe it was pure stupidity.

What was he doing over here? Shouldn't he be on Tom's property? She sent the dog an image of her talking to Tom, petting Sam, telling him to sit.

Sam cocked his head as his growls stopped. Vonda pushed the images harder, her petting his head as he sat. Sitting was good, he wanted to sit, he didn't want to attack. Attacking bad, sitting good.

Sam sat.

She pictured the house and sent it to Sam. Unfortunately, the house reminded her of Tom, and her blood ran hot, her sex swelling. Sam whined and stood.

Eww, yuck. He wouldn't dare. She ventured a glance under the dog's hindquarters. Whew. Neutered.

She snarled again, trying the house pictures once

more. Sam sat; the tip of his tail wagging and Vonda saw Tom sitting at a table with a girl of around ten, the scent of fear rolling off him. Vonda closed her eyes, shaking her head. A dog sent her pictures?

She'd never had that happen before. But why shouldn't it, dogs were distant cousins and all canines possessed the ability for telepathy. Which was why dog training came so naturally to her. She pictured what the dog should do until the animal understood which sound went with the picture. However, no dog had sent any image other than chasing critters back to her.

Maybe she could only communicate with them while in wolf form. If being a werewolf only came with a how-to manual, things would be a lot easier.

Tom's fear, as seen through Sam's eyes, strode through her brain, triggering a like response in her. Sam's ward was in trouble, she had to help. Wait a minute; Tom didn't belong to Sam, which was the whole root of the trouble in that relationship.

Vonda shook her head. It didn't matter at the moment who was in charge, Tom or Sam, all that mattered was that Tom was in trouble, something was wrong. Vonda probed into Sam's memories, seeing nothing to cause fear in Tom. His daughter was smiling, but something was wrong.

What? Sam had ducked out the dog door, smelling her scent even across the distance. He hadn't wanted her kill, he'd wanted her.

And now she had to help him.

Sam barked once, signaling he understood her decision to help him and took off across the darkened pasture, heading toward the house, Vonda following.

****

"Hey Dad, look what I did in art class." Elizabeth held up a canvas with a picture of the mountains.

"You painted that?"

She nodded. "Yep. Whatcha think?"

"Wow, girl. You're quite the little artist." Tom smiled, impressed with her picture. Who knew his daughter drew like that?

"Daaadddyyy." She slapped a hand down on the kitchen table. "I'm NOT a little girl. I'm almost grown."

Problem was she spoke the truth. Amazing how time flew. He'd swear yesterday he first held her in his arms, her tiny fists balled, her face red and grimacing. She sat at the table, her features identical to his, her hair, though, the dark brown of Anita's, a girl on the cusp of adolescence. What would he do with a teenage girl? Weren't there things only a woman could tell her?

He really needed to start dating. If not for himself then for his daughter. She needed a mom. A mom like Vonda.

Visions of tanned legs wrapped around his waist while he drove into her, again and again, harder, faster, rushed through his brain. What was it about that woman that got him hard while he cooked dinner? There was nothing sexy about raw meat.

Tom flipped the burger on his indoor grill and continued his conversation with Elizabeth.

"Yep, you're growing up. Pretty soon you'll be able to cook for me while I sit and watch you."

"Don't be ridiculous, Daddy. I can't cook."

Tom laughed. Elizabeth always said that. She looked so peaceful sitting at the table, doing her homework. Nothing at all like his vision, where a huge man held her, her face dripping blood from a cut on her head, her eyes wide, as she struggled in the man's grip.

Just thinking of what he saw gave Tom chills.

"Daddy, it's burning!"

So it was. Tom flipped the burger, shooting Elizabeth an apologetic smile. "A little charcoal never hurt anyone, honey."

"Whatever." She waved a hand, returning to her books.

Would he be able to keep her safe? Where was he in that vision? That man he saw was huge, like a steroid-crazed wrestler, and Tom was no lightweight.

Why...how? Tom's visions always came true. Or at least they had when he was a child; he hadn't tried to see anything since he saw his mother's death a day before she died. Now he needed to learn how to stop that man from getting Elizabeth.

The man had been in the house, he realized with a start as he flipped the burger onto a plate. He put a raw meat patty on the grill. How did that man get into his house?

The scariest thing was, what had happened to him? Was he dead? Why wasn't he helping Elizabeth? Once caught, that man would be dead, that much he knew for sure. Murdering the son of a bitch sounded like a good idea.

"Hey, Daddy," Elizabeth's voice dropped him into the here and now. "It's a full moon. You think another steer is going to die?"

"I don't know, hon."

Unknowingly, she managed to derail his morbid thoughts onto another little problem his ranch had. As if vandals breaking fences to get to his daughter wasn't enough bad luck, for the past three months something, probably a wolf, had been gnawing on his herd. Each full moon brought another dead steer. If he didn't know any better, he'd think it was a werewolf, but those only existed in folklore. They couldn't really exist.

If he stuck like barbed wire to the herd for the next three nights, he might catch the wolf, but what was the loss of another steer when compared to his daughter? Nope, he'd stay home where he could watch her. Maybe next month he'd catch the wolf, if the thing gnawed its way through another cow tonight.

"Daddy, where'd Sam go?" Elizabeth looked at him, her amber eyes reflecting the light. His mother's eyes. Although the color was oddly like Vonda's.

Damn. He had to think of her again. The fantasy started playing, an endless loop in his mind. Double damn. Elizabeth had asked him a question, he should be thinking with the head on his shoulders. What the fuck was wrong with him tonight?

"I'm not sure, honey. Why don't you clear off the table and set it? I'm almost done over here."

Dinner, Tom. Think of dinner not Vonda. Dinner. What about strawberries used to paint chocolate down her firm flesh, leading to...

He flipped the overcooked burger onto the plate, turned off the grill and slammed the spatula onto the cabinet. Elizabeth squeaked.

"Sorry, honey. It slipped." Slipped in and out of hot, wet, warm flesh. In and out, over and over...

"You okay, Daddy?"

"Um, yeah. I have to go pee. I'll be right back."

Hoping Elizabeth didn't see the bulge in his pants, he walked to the bathroom and slumped against the door. Taking himself in hand, he grasped the length of his dick and stroked. Once, twice and he came over his hand, teeth gritting against the pleasure. Well, whatcha know, the damn thing still worked.

Grabbing a tissue, he cleaned up the mess. He really needed to get control of himself. He couldn't just run to the bathroom every five minutes like a horny teenager. Elizabeth would know something was wrong and this was one conversation he didn't feel like having.

Yeah, honey, Daddy has the hots for the dog trainer, which causes him to have to jack off every so often, but it's good to know the ole dick still works. Uh-huh. Right.

He finished washing his hands and was reaching for the towel when the lights went out. What the hell? No storm or high winds were in the area. Maybe the fuse shorted for the bathroom. He'd have to go check.

Layla growled. Tom's heart rate jacked up a notch. He'd owned the dog fourteen years and never once had she growled. Barked, yes, growled, never. Until now.

The doorknob slipped in his wet grasp. He used a corner of his shirt to twist the knob, managing to barely turn it when he heard Elizabeth scream. The scream died as flesh met flesh and a crash sounded. Oh, God, no. His nightmare had just begun.

Tom yanked the door open, rushing into the scene from his vision. The room was dark, dappled in moonlight filtering through the blinds, unlike his vision where the room seemed lighter.

He blinked, rage consuming him. When he opened his eyes, the room seemed brighter and he smelled blood and the sharp tang of terror. A chair lay on the floor, papers scattered everywhere. A huge man with a shaved head and more tats than a prisoner held Elizabeth, one hand clamped over her mouth, one muscle-bulging arm wrapped around her waist. Her feet pummeled his shins, but the blows meant nothing to the man.

Tom felt his lips peel over his teeth as a red film settled across his eyes. That son of a bitch hurt his daughter. He heard an inhuman howl echo through the kitchen and the skinhead's eyebrows skimmed skyward. For a minute Tom wondered how Layla could make a noise like that, and then he realized it didn't come from the dog, it came from him.

Odd, but then no one had ever tried to kidnap his little girl before.

His limbs tingled as if he'd stuck his finger in an electrical outlet, energy pulsing through them. His muscles felt like they were growing, lengthening, becoming stronger. His teeth, especially the incisors, ached. His throat quivered as that inhuman howl broke out again. Elizabeth's eyes widened.

He focused on her, noting how her eyes glanced behind him as she struggled to speak, her words muffled incoherently. A rush of air to his right caused him to turn, but he was too late. A heavy weight struck his head and he crumpled.

He heard Elizabeth's muffled yells as he struggled against the darkness in his head. The front door banged shut and Tom knew he'd failed her. Darkness consumed him.

Chapter 3

Vonda saw the house from a distance. *Uh-oh.* It looked as if she'd been eating cattle from her newest client. That couldn't be a good thing. Maybe Tom hadn't noticed. It could happen.

Sam trotted along beside her, glancing at her occasionally from the corner of his eye. She hadn't gathered anything else from his canine brain in their journey to the house. Just like a male to be the silent type.

In the distance she saw the house, shining like a lighthouse to a weary traveler. Her steps slowed. She was in wolf form and would be until morning. What would Tom do when he saw her? Shoot her? What was she thinking to trail after Sam like this?

Sam looked at her and Vonda felt his mind touch hers.

Hurry. Fear. Help.

Sam had a point. Even from this distance something seemed off. A discord in the harmony of nature. What the hell. If Tom needed her help she was all for it. Maybe afterward he'd repay her with sex. Yeah. That sounded like a great idea. He might be a bit freaked out when she changed, but he'd know she helped him and he'd throw her on the bed, thrusting inside her, and…

The lights shut off at the house, effectively

throwing her out of her fantasy. Vonda stopped, startled by the sudden loss of light. Sam's ears cocked forward as he sniffed the air. Vonda dragged a deep sniff in too, smelling the scents of evening along with a new scent.

Her nostrils flared. What was that? The smell triggered a response in the wolf's brain that resonated in her body. Despite the fact she had never smelled that scent before, she knew what it was. It smelled like her. A mixture of magic and evergreen.

Werewolves.

What were werewolves doing here? Who cared about that, would they want to meet her? Where were they?

She scanned the perimeter of the house, looking for wolves, but all she saw were two men, one of them carrying what looked like a bundle of blankets in his arm. The bundle jerked and even from where she sat Vonda could see the man's muscles bulge as he tightened his grip on his load. Sam growled.

Elizabeth.

Vonda looked at Sam and back at the men as they walked toward a car parked along the main road. She breathed in, thankful the wind carried the men's scents to her and not hers to them. Sure enough, three different scents slammed into her nose, two werewolves and one scared girl. She should have picked up on that earlier.

Sam darted through the grass, heading toward the men, Vonda following. This was worse than she thought. She hadn't imagined this when Sam came to her, telling of Tom's fear.

These men were like her, she knew it, she smelled them. So why were they in human form? How could a werewolf stay in human form when the moon shone full and bright?

She'd have to ask, after she knocked their asses down for stealing a little girl. What kind of perverts were they? Taking a kid like that. Where was Tom?

Vonda didn't care to think where he might be, or the condition he was in. She'd find Tom after she stopped these bastards.

Legs churning, she overtook Sam, passing him as if he were a turtle on a sunny day. If she didn't get a move on those perverts would have that girl in their car. Good thing she ran faster than the average wolf, although that steer in her stomach slowed her down.

The giant man carrying Tom's daughter laid her, blankets and all, in the backseat, and wrapped the seatbelt around her, while the other one got behind the wheel. Trying not to puke—not even a wolf should exercise after eating—Vonda sprinted toward the giant.

The car's engine turned over, headlights splashing over the ground, blinding her. She veered out of the bright path, noting the giant stood watching her, one hand on the car door.

Vonda leapt, aiming for his throat. He took a step toward her, catching her around the neck and throwing her to the side. Vonda landed with a thud, the air knocked out of her. The vibration of his steps ran across her skin as he walked toward her but it was a little hard to move when she couldn't breathe.

As quickly as it left, the air rushed into her lungs and she rolled, standing up even though her legs felt like they would collapse. Ears back, she snarled at Giant Pervert as his voice resonated in her ears.

"Where the fuck did you come from?"

"What is it, Big G?" The man from the car hopped

out, staring at them.

She saw Sam leap at the man, slamming him into the car frame. The man let out a screech as he hit, the noise turning into a growl, followed by a yip.

Sam, danger! Get Tom!

A beefy hand clamped on the ruff of her neck, lifting her into the air. She put all four feet against GP's chest and pushed as she snapped at his wrist.

Blood gushed from his arm and he dropped her with a curse. She darted out of his reach, eyeing him for any sudden movement.

Who the hell are you and why aren't you a wolf? In case you didn't notice the bloody moon's full.

"Someone needs to teach you a lesson, bitch. Who's your pack leader?"

Don't have one. Why are you taking Elizabeth?

"Why don't you have a pack leader?"

Because you're the only werewolf I've met. Now give me back the girl and no one will get hurt.

His teeth flashed. "Funny one, aren't you. In case you didn't notice you're a bit outnumbered. And you didn't answer my question, who's your leader?"

Maybe you're just deaf. I said I'm my own leader, I answer to no one. Let me have Elizabeth, you perv.

His brows carved a row in his forehead as he ignored her request. "Seriously? You be telling the truth about no leader?"

Vonda stared at him.

"Well, well. Isn't this interesting. Hey Jace, the bitch here has no leader."

Vonda ventured a glance at Jace, and immediately wished she hadn't when she saw Sam lying in the grass. She growled. Jace put up his hands.

"Hey, now, he attacked me. He's not dead; don't get your fur all ruffled."

"What should we do with her? She shouldn't be left alone." GP looked worried.

I'm fine. Just give me back the girl. You perverted or something? What do you want with a little girl?

"I'm not no perv. That's sick. You don't understand our ways."

Then explain them. That should be interesting to hear, after all, she'd been waiting most of her life to hear some explanation of what she was and maybe the ensuing conversation would give Elizabeth enough time to unroll the blankets and jump out of the car.

Unfortunately, Jace possessed more brains than his skinhead friend and figured that little bit of info out on his own. Dammit.

"Big G, leave the bitch. We'll find her later. Get in the car before things go to hell."

In Vonda's opinion, things had already arrived. How much worse could they get?

Jace gestured at Big G and slipped behind the wheel.

Big G scratched his bald head. "I hate leaving you here. Wolves should run together. Don't worry. We'll come back for you." He walked to the car and waggled his fingers at her.

Vonda followed, trotting to the driver's side. She might be able to open the door and pull Elizabeth out. But again, her plan was foiled by Jace who gunned the engine before Big G had time to shut his door.

Vonda started running, chasing after the car for all she was worth, mortified she just let a child be kidnapped by a couple of werewolves. At least she had their scents imprinted on her brain. She'd be able to track them.

****

Tom woke with a headache, a constant pounding in his ears. Why was he on the floor? And then it rushed back with a sickening thud, a crushing weight on his ribs. He'd failed Elizabeth. They took his daughter and he couldn't stop them. Tears stung his eyes as his breath caught in his throat. Her life from infancy until now flashed in his mind, each picture generating another invisible sucker punch to the chest.

The cops. He had to call the cops.

Slamming his palms against the floor, he pushed himself to all fours, the room spinning as if he were drunk. As he leveraged himself to his feet, the room stopped its merry-go-round dance. Why was the room so bright?

Light poured in from between the blinds, flooding the room. Had he really been unconscious for the remainder of the night? He heard a motor rev and ran toward the window, peering between the slats of the blinds, his eyes blinking in the car's headlights.

Elizabeth must be in that car. Screw the police. If the kidnappers were sitting outside, he would take care of them himself. It wasn't too late to kill the bastards that took her.

He ran to the door, and saw the gun case with his rifle standing against the wall. Yeah, capping the bastards in their asses sounded like a great idea. Problem was, the case was locked and damn it if he couldn't remember where the keys were. Like he had time to find the fuckers.

Wrapping his hand in his shirttail, he slammed his

fist through the glass, imagining it was the kidnappers' faces. Shards sprinkled around his feet. Tom grabbed some ammo and with shaking hands slammed it into the rifle and pulled the bolt.

Locked and loaded.

The door took longer to open than it should have, but then it fell open with a squeak and a thud and Tom bolted through it. His head pounding, bile choking his throat, he jumped off the porch and took off at a dead sprint after the car.

Was that a wolf chasing the car? Tom blinked, shaking his head. What the hell? He must have taken a harder hit than he thought.

Legs pumping, he ran faster than he thought himself capable of. He had to catch them, had to get Elizabeth back. And what was that weight in his hands?

Oh, yeah. The rifle. Shit for brains, he could fire on the motherfuckers. Except if he did that, the car could flip and Elizabeth could die. But he had to stop them and chasing after the car on foot wasn't working. How to stop them?

He had a truck. Yeah, the truck. Four wheels chased faster than two feet.

His lungs burned with the exertion, but he couldn't rest, couldn't rest until Elizabeth was back in his arms.

Tom took off, sprinting back to the truck. Halfway there, he heard footsteps behind him. His heart picked up the pace, triple-timing it as he realized the wolf followed him.

Shit, he didn't have time to be eaten by a wolf. He needed to save his daughter.

If he got to the truck, he could leave before the wolf caught him.

Keys, he needed his keys. Neither of his pockets contained them. He remembered his rifle, but left his keys who knows where? How could he chase after Elizabeth without his truck? Fly? Stupid idiot. And the wolf was still behind him keeping pace, stalking him.

Tom darted behind the truck, aimed his rifle at the wolf and tried to get his breathing under control.

****

Circling around, Vonda followed Tom back as he sprinted toward the house. She saw Sam push himself to his feet, his body undulating, his collar jingling with the motion.

Thank God he didn't seem hurt. She reached out with her mind, rummaged around in his thoughts, learning he was sore, but not badly injured.

Since Sam was okay, her attention turned back to Tom, only to see him on the other side of his truck, his rifle pointed at her. Oh, shit.

Tom, it's me Vonda. Put the rifle down!

Like her thoughts would help. Most humans couldn't understand her telepathically. But she had to try. Being shot was not high on her to-do list.

****

Tom felt a buzz like insects in his head and heard words. *Tom, it's me Vonda. Put the rifle down!*

Oh, yeah. He definitely got hit harder than he thought.

But what if that really was Vonda? Okay, he didn't get hit that hard, like a woman could turn into a wolf. He tightened the grip on the rifle, his chest pumping like a bellows.

Tom, please! You don't believe it, but it's true. It's Vonda, please don't kill me. Please. Shit, he doesn't hear me.

What if it was Vonda? The blood that wasn't pounding in his head rushed to his dick at the thought of her. Great, just great. Kidnappers just drove off with his daughter, he sees a wolf, hears voices in his head, and gets a hard-on. What kind of a fucking freak was he?

Why not humor the voices? How much worse could it get?

"Fine. If you're really Vonda take two steps to the right, sit and wait right there."

The wolf walked two steps to the right, eyes on him and sat. Damn.

He had no time for this shit. Each minute he spent aiming the rifle at the wolf, his brain obviously tripping on a hemorrhage, was one more minute those fuckers had his daughter.

To hell with that. The wolf was either Vonda or it wasn't. Some things you just had to trust to fate no matter how unbelievable.

"Get your ass in the truck while I get the keys."

Not waiting to see what the wolf would do, Tom lowered the rifle and darted up the steps into the house. Layla poked her head out from behind the couch. Ignoring her, he grabbed his cell phone and keys off the table by the door. Spinning around, he almost tripped over Sam as the dog came into the house.

Cursing, he side-stepped Sam and yanked the door shut. The wolf sat by the passenger door of the truck, looking over her shoulder at him.

"Are you really Vonda?" he whispered.

In the flesh.

He paused, trying to stop breathing like a race

horse. If that wasn't Vonda, his ass was pretty much screwed. One foot after another, his breath caught in his throat, he walked toward the wolf. *Dear God, let her be Vonda.* One thing finally went well on this hellacious evening—the wolf didn't bite him and jumped straight into the truck when he opened the door.

Okay, that went well. The only thing left for him was to get in the truck and drive hell-bent after the fuckers who had his daughter. Provided the wolf in his truck didn't eat him first.

What the hell had he been thinking?

Tom slammed a fist on the hood of the truck as he walked around to the driver's side. Yanking open the door he was greeted by a lolling tongue and a lot of overgrown pearly whites. Was that blood on her muzzle? His heart skipped a beat.

Oh, get in already. We went through this earlier.

Tom took a deep breath and placed the rifle on the gun rack before sliding behind the wheel. He fumbled with the keys, two tries later he had the key in the ignition and the engine turned. Adrenaline raced through his veins. The bastards who took his daughter would pay for it. He'd make sure of that.

Shifting into reverse, he backed out of the driveway, gunning the engine when he dropped it into drive.

"Which way?" he growled and then blinked at the sound.

What was up with those strange noises coming out of his mouth? He sounded almost animalistic. Well, hell, he felt animalistic and would go medieval on their asses once he found the kidnappers. What did they want with Elizabeth? He shuddered, thinking about what his daughter must be going through as he white-knuckled the steering wheel.

He'd always protected her; what would she think of him now? How would she be able to look up to him when he let her be taken?

You didn't let her be taken. They took her. There's a difference.

Tom whipped his head to the right, staring at Vonda.

"How the hell did you know what I was thinking?"

You weren't thinking it, you said it. I heard you.

"Nope. It was in my head." Was he actually arguing with a wolf? Even if said wolf was the sexiest woman he'd seen. His groin throbbed thinking about Vonda's hair, her beautiful amber eyes, her hot body. How the hell could he be thinking of sex at a time like this?

You think I'm sexy?

"You need to work on that telepathy thing."

Sorry. I usually talk to wolves, not humans. You're the only human I've been able to talk to like this. They can't understand me. I'm surprised you can.

"Yeah, I can understand you just fine. The problem is that you're reading my mind."

Well, I wouldn't be reading it if you weren't broadcasting it all over the place. Seems to me like you're talking. Hey, stop! I need to get out and smell for tracks at the corner.

Tom slammed the brakes; thankful he had just turned the corner and wasn't going fast. Vonda waited, staring at Tom. Tom stared back. If she needed to scent the tracks, she better get out.

Do you see any hands over here? One paw dangled

in the air.

Tom reached across the seat and pushed the door open. Vonda leapt out and put her nose on the ground. She sniffed all four corners of the road, then stuck her nose in the air and walked around the corners. Her nostrils quivered as she breathed.

As he watched Vonda make her rounds, Tom wished she'd hurry. This whole sniff-out-the-bad-guys routine took too long. He tapped his fingers against the steering wheel, feeling his blood pressure rise the longer Vonda sniffed the ground. Enough already. He could have driven to the Canadian border and back in the time it took her to sniff around the road.

After what the dashboard clock claimed was only two minutes—he obviously needed to take it in for service since it wasn't working right—she trotted back to the truck. The seat dipped as Vonda landed next to him, a wolfish grin on her face. She glanced at the door, then him, one paw waving back and forth.

He grunted, reached around her and shut the door, holding in the chills that inched their way to his low back as his arm brushed her muzzle.

Head to the right, their scent is the strongest in that direction. Stop if you come to cross streets.

Tom shifted into drive and stomped on the gas. On this stretch of road, heading in this direction there were no cross streets for miles, which made it easier to track he supposed. Thinking about tracking Elizabeth gave him fresh chills as to what those men, particularly the giant one, wanted with his daughter.

"Why would they take Elizabeth? Why would they come into the house and take her? It's not like she was on a street alone or something. What kind of freaks break into a house and take a little girl? I don't even know them!" He slammed his hand on the steering wheel.

They're werewolves. Like me.

Tom's lip curled, exposing his teeth. "You know them?"

What? You think I hang with kidnappers?

"Until tonight I didn't even realize werewolves existed."

It was a surprise for me too.

"What do you mean?"

****

Vonda sighed. She might as well tell him. He was stuck with her until they caught up to Elizabeth. And judging by the whine of the engine, that shouldn't be too much longer.

I grew up in a foster home and didn't know werewolves existed until I turned into one when I was thirteen.

Tom faced her, mouth agape. "That must've been hard."

You have no idea. My foster parents thought I was doing drugs or something since I snuck out of the house every full moon. Figured it was easier for them to think I was snorting coke than to have them see me turn into a wolf.

"Yeah, I can imagine. That would be weird. Can you change at will?"

Vonda shook her head. *Nope. Only on the day of the full moon, the day before and the day after. I turn when the sun sets on those days.*

Vonda licked her lips. What would Tom do if she ran her tongue over his ear? Maybe he'd reciprocate in kind. Yeah, she could deal with that. After the ear, he'd move on down...

Tom turned to her, eyes raking her. She smelled the scent of arousal swimming through the truck's cab, thick and heady. Hot damn, he actually found the wolf attractive. Not like she cared at the moment with the mating heat coursing through her body. She'd take him any way she could, but maybe this relationship wouldn't end like the other one.

Tom faced forward, hands tightening on the wheel.

"Look up there. Are those taillights?" One finger pointed straight ahead.

Vonda looked down the road, squinting. Yep, definitely taillights. Her lips peeled back from her teeth.

I think we've caught the bastards.

Chapter 4

Tom flipped the lights off as he rolled to a stop. He jumped out and tried the gate the kidnappers had driven through.

Locked.

The red of the taillights disappeared in the woods, swallowed in the shadows, leaving Tom alone with his failure.

He kicked the gate a couple of times before yanking on it.

Keep that up and the whole world will know we're here.

Vonda trotted to where he stood fighting the gate.

"Well, what do you suggest? I can't just Superman over the damn thing." The gate stood at least seven feet tall, a wrought iron monstrosity, attaching to an equally impressive fence. No footholds to be seen. Whoever lived here didn't raise cattle.

And Elizabeth was behind those formidable walls.

We can go under it. See, it doesn't go too far into the ground. Look at that rabbit tunnel underneath.

Tom looked to where Vonda gestured with her nose. The light seemed brighter than normal, and he saw the small hole a rabbit had dug under the fence.

"Well, what are you waiting for? Dig!"

Vonda shook her head and trotted over to the rabbit tunnel. Dirt flew as the hole deepened. What a woman, um, wolf. Tom ran back to the truck and grabbed his rifle. By the time he returned, Vonda stood on the other side of the fence.

Hope you fit through. I tried to dig it large enough for you.

Tom poked the rifle through the space between the bars before lowering himself into the hole. His head poked out the other side of the fence easily, but the rest of him didn't want to pass through.

A scream died in his throat, the only sound an escaped grunt.

Back up and I'll dig some from this side.

Tom pulled back and let Vonda work. This time he was able to pull himself through. Picking up the rifle, he followed Vonda as she led him through the woods.

The road wound between trees for what seemed like miles. Time crept forward, slower than Layla in the winter. Probably because they took the scenic route through the woods instead of trotting on the dirt-packed road. Less chance of being seen. Hopefully.

At least it gave Tom plenty of time to think, to plan new ways of killing the bastards who took his daughter. Shooting was too clean. So was snapping their necks. He should have brought the axe.

They're in the clearing.

"Huh?"

Shh! Just think it. Do you really want them to hear you?

Tom glared at her. She stared back, amber eyes unblinking. Brave women were sexy.

Canines gleamed in the darkness as Vonda stood a little straighter.

Damn. He'd projected thoughts he hadn't meant to.

Again. Well, he was new at this telepathy thing. He planned on getting better at it once he had Elizabeth back. Then he could concentrate on Vonda. Until then visions of long legs wrapped around his waist and amber eyes glowing in the moonlight were relegated to the back of his mind.

Dropping to the ground, Tom crawled toward the clearing, Vonda following.

Wonder if they can smell me.

Why...Tom started, remembered why and shut his mental trap. *Can't you mask your scent?*

Her head tilted to the side as she stared at him. *See any dead animals around?*

What does that have to do with it?

Vonda shook her head. *In order for me to mask my scent, I need to roll on something dead.*

Before Tom could think a reply to that little pleasantry, they arrived at the clearing. Numerous men, women and wolves—which he assumed to be of the were variety—stood huddled in a circle, staring in the middle of ring. Too many for him to take out, even if Vonda managed to take a couple down.

Where was Elizabeth? He looked around the clearing, surprised by how light it seemed. The moon was full, but it should be shadowed in the woods, clearing or not. Tom looked to the tops of the trees, searched for lights and saw none. Maybe there was something he couldn't see that reflected the light, making the shadows disappear.

Or maybe his eyes had adjusted so well to the dark that the dark now seemed light.

A person moved, allowing him a glimpse into the circle, a glimpse into what they hid, and a glimpse at his daughter.

Elizabeth huddled on the ground, knees to her chest, face buried in her knees.

And then the person moved again and his glimpse vanished.

Tom felt an almost overwhelming need to kill them all. His heart pounded in his chest, beat in his head, pulsed in his teeth, down his throat.

An unearthly sound echoed in his ears, turning every head in the clearing to him.

Like he cared.

They had his daughter, his only child, and they would die.

He sprang forward.

Chapter 5

Vonda turned to Tom as he howled. Howled. Since when did men howl?

Okay, maybe in the heat of passion, but nothing like what he let out. Her bones felt like ants crawling through them, small tingles burning deep.

She took a deep breath and gasped. What the...

Tom sprang from where he laid, muscles bulging. Vonda tried to reach for him, remembering at the last second she had no hands to pull him back.

Tom, no! Wait!

Of course he didn't. Since when did men listen to a woman? And he'd left his rifle behind. Brilliant. Fight a bunch of werewolves barehanded.

If what she smelled on him was accurate, and her nose didn't lie, he might have a better chance than she thought.

By now the startled werewolves flocked around Tom, while Elizabeth screamed, "Daddy!"

She should help Tom fight, she really should, but fighting was so not her thing. Sneaking, now that she was good at. She could sneak right around the clearing while Tom distracted them all and try to free Elizabeth. Two women stood by the girl, obviously guarding her.

Vonda slunk through the shadows, blending into the night, until she stood about thirty feet from Elizabeth. The girl still screamed for her father, but from the looks of things, Tom had lost. She didn't have much time left to do what she planned. Thankfully she had learned while running with the wolves how to speak telepathically to one wolf and not the whole pack.

Elizabeth, I'm behind you in the woods. Vonda projected the thought into the girl's mind, praying Elizabeth could hear her.

The girl's head whipped around, eyes frantically searching.

Score one for the wolf. Now to convince her.

I'm a friend of your dad's and here to help. Start crawling to me. I'll distract them.

But Dad—

Let's get you out first.

Vonda picked up a stick with her mouth and pitched it. She heard it hit, but the two guards didn't. Shit. Quick, Plan B. She howled.

That got their attention.

Hey, Bitch. To your right. You wanna piece of this? She turned and stuck her tail into the clearing, waggling it.

One of the guards gestured for the other one to check it out. The woman trotted right, the other one watching her.

Elizabeth, change of plans. Run left, quick, go!

Elizabeth, bless her heart, jumped up and hauled ass. Tom really needed to put the girl in track.

"Hey, she's getting away!"

Elizabeth was to the edge of the clearing before the wolves started moving. Vonda circled around, shocked she could feel the wolves' surprise and indecision over whether to stay with Tom or chase Elizabeth. Half stayed, half chased.

Damn.

Before she made it to Elizabeth, the same giant who had stolen the girl came from behind a tree and grabbed her again. Vonda leapt, slamming into Big G and Elizabeth, taking them both down. Elizabeth scrambled out, and Vonda went for Big G's throat.

She never made it.

A hand grabbed the scruff of her neck, shaking. Vonda knew she should submit because the hand was attached to what smelled like a dominant leader, but submitting meant letting them take Elizabeth and Tom and she couldn't do it. She snarled, turning her head to bite.

A wave of power washed over her, power she had never before felt, a power that froze the bite on her lips. Vonda looked up, right into the face of one of the women who had guarded Elizabeth in the clearing.

Pack leader. Alpha. Submit.

Vonda snarled. Another wave of power crashed over her and she felt her body start changing. What the hell? The moon was still out. She fought against the power that coursed over her, through her, trying to force the human half of her back into hiding.

For the first time in her life, she fought to stay in the wolf's body. With everything she had, she concentrated on maintaining the wolf, until her vision narrowed to the tall, athletic, brown-haired woman holding her scruff. Just the two of them, locked in a battle of wills.

The woman's eyes widened, then narrowed as Vonda felt more power slam into her. Vonda imaged a wall between her and the pack leader, a wall that blocked all power, a wall that let her remain a wolf.

The hand slipped from her neck, allowing Vonda a toe-hold in the struggle.

Submit, dammit! The words reverberated in her head, willing her to lie on her side, the urge almost overpowering.

Like hell. She was too far into this fight to back down now.

I...don't...think so. I want...Elizabeth...and Tom.

You don't understand what you ask for.

Then...why...don't...you...explain.

The woman screamed, throwing her hand toward Big G, who cowered on the ground. The power beating against Vonda's body suddenly lifted as Big G shrieked, his body exploding into a wolf.

Holy shit.

Elizabeth screamed. The wolves and humans dropped to the ground, rolling on their sides. Vonda fought to remain standing, the clash of power and her own struggle against the leader leaving her drained, her legs shaky.

The last note of Elizabeth's scream dripped from the trees, coating them with silence. The pack leader's chest heaved, her frustration evident in her scent.

"Who the hell are you?" Hands fisted on her waist, she glared at Vonda.

Who the hell do you think you are, kidnapping a little girl?

"You didn't answer my question."

You're not answering mine.

The hands dropped to her sides as she took a breath. "Are you challenging me?"

Words like ice lanced through Vonda's veins and the just-returning forest noises went silent. Some deeper meaning to the pack leader's words existed, but for the life of her, Vonda didn't know what it was. Time to bluff.

All I want is Elizabeth and Tom back. If you call that challenging, then I guess so.

"Does your pack do things so much differently?"

What do you mean?

"Does your pack not raise pups from interspecies unions?"

Interspecies unions? Could she sound any more stupid? What did the woman mean by that one?

"Surely you can smell it on her. Elizabeth belongs to us, she's one of us. Tom never changed, he can't raise her. How would he explain what she's going through when she changes? It's in Elizabeth's best interests to live with the pack."

Whoa, Nelly. Elizabeth was a werewolf? Vonda glanced to where the girl stood, mesmerized by the alpha. At least she stood instead of groveling around on the ground like the rest of the pack. That was a good thing, right?

Tom's a werewolf?

"You really didn't know, did you?" The woman bent closer, sniffing Vonda's neck. "Who are you? You don't belong to us."

Vonda side-stepped, but the alpha grabbed the scruff of her neck again. Geez, if the pack leader didn't cease and desist with that scruff-grabbing routine Vonda would have to bite her.

"She told us she had no leader."

Vonda darted her eyes in the direction of the voice. Jace crawled into her line of vision. *Uh-oh. Not good.* She had the distinct impression not having a leader was a bad thing.

"Really?" Ms. Pack Leader gave her a curious look. "How did that happen?"

The fight left Vonda. She'd always wanted to meet another werewolf, but didn't know how. Chat rooms didn't cater to the real thing and she didn't know where else to look. Couldn't ask anyone either without running the risk of men in little white suits heading her way. She smelled frustration and curiosity from Ms. PL, not hatred. Maybe these wolves knew why she was what she was. But first she had to ensure Tom and Elizabeth's safety.

What did you do with Tom?

"You like to avoid questions. Fine, I'll answer some of yours but you owe me in return, got it?"

Vonda nodded.

"Tom will be fine. I'm not sure why he's so upset over the matter. He should know that we mean only the best for Elizabeth."

But you kidnapped her and knocked him out! How could that be the best for her?

"Kidnapped? Tom's mother should have explained all this," she waggled her fingers back and forth, "to him before she died. He knew we'd be coming for Elizabeth."

Um, hate to be the one to tell you, but I think someone dropped the ball on that one.

The PL dropped Vonda's scruff and turned on Jace and Big G. "What did you tell Tom when you fetched the girl?"

Jace dropped on his side. "We was supposed to tell him something?"

Vonda watched PL practice her deep breathing

exercises. Maybe she counted to ten. In four different languages. Vonda would've just smacked the werewolf, but obviously this woman ran things another way.

"Thanks to my enforcers, it seems we owe Tom an apology."

She marched over to the clearing, Vonda hot on her heels, Elizabeth staying put like a good submissive. Tom lay on the ground, two wolves lying beside him. Vonda ran over to him, licking his face.

His eyes opened. The pain in their depths made something twist deep inside Vonda. He hurt and she wanted to kill the cause of it.

"Daddy!" Elizabeth came running as Tom struggled to sit. Apparently the girl wasn't as submissive as she'd seemed.

Throwing her arms around his shoulders, she buried her face in his neck as Tom's arms surrounded her with the grip of a desperate man.

Not intending to barge in on their reunion, but in case PL decided to take Elizabeth back, Vonda edged her way closer to Tom, close enough for her fur to brush against his arm. Probably not the best position to take seeing how even that littlest of touches sparked another bout of the mating heat.

The alpha knelt in front of Tom. "Seems we owe you an apology. We assumed you knew we would come for Elizabeth. But it looks like your mother never told you about herself or about you. Elizabeth belongs with us, the pack. You didn't change but she will."

****

Tom looked at the woman, willing breath into his lungs. Change? What the hell did she mean, change? But one glance around the clearing told him what she meant. Even if he didn't want to believe it, he knew deep down he was different. It didn't take a genius to realize the sixth sense type of thing he experienced his entire life didn't happen to everyone. Being a werewolf, and a genetically defective one at that, never crossed his mind.

Breathe, Tom. In through the nose, out through the mouth.

Now that air managed to flood his lungs, he wanted nothing more than to laugh. Wild, hysterical laughter that meant craziness knocked at his door.

Well, hell, laughter was the best medicine, right?

The writer of that cliché obviously didn't have his problem.

"Huh?" squeaked out. Embarrassing. So much for sounding coherent.

The woman sighed. "Werewolves, Tom. You should have changed, but didn't. Sometimes it happens. Usually one that does not change doesn't have a child that does, but Elizabeth will change."

"How do you know that?" Goody for him, his voice didn't sound like a pubescent boy.

"We can smell it on her. You have a similar scent. Rather surprising since you don't change." She shrugged. "But the point is that Elizabeth needs to be raised by us. How else will she know how to be a wolf?"

Tom's arms tightened around Elizabeth. They'd pretty much proved he'd lose the fight, but that wouldn't stop him from trying again.

Um, excuse me. Vonda interjected. *But why can't she just live with Tom and you can check in on her? Wouldn't that be better for her? To, like, live with her father?*

Tom and the alpha stared at her. Why hadn't he thought of that? His first reaction had been to fight, not talk it out. God, he loved that wolf, um, woman.

The alpha blinked a couple of times, clearly mulling over Vonda's suggestion. She looked at Elizabeth held in Tom's white-knuckled grasp.

The damn bitch best go for the idea. Tom held his breath seeing as it wasn't doing much good going in and out of his mouth.

He watched as her head tilted to the side. Emotions played across her face as her eyes drifted to various pack members.

Tom heard what sounded like thousands of bees buzzing in his skull. He shook his head, but the sound didn't go away. Vonda's head turned as she looked around the pack with the alpha.

No way. But after everything else that happened tonight, why not? He focused on the noise in his head, turning the cacophony into a single strand of conversation. Check him out, eavesdropping on a private conversation.

He should have remained ignorant. Because who wants to know what the gossip is saying about you?

Seems like there was some debate on who the lucky wolf that got to visit Elizabeth was. More debate on if Vonda's idea should even happen, which took longer than he'd like. Back to the wolf who got to visit Elizabeth—of course it was the brown-haired woman. And, whoa Nelly, were they now deciding who he slept with?

Like hell if they thought they could decide that. The only one he wanted was Vonda.

The buzzing stopped as most of the pack, including Vonda, turned to stare at him.

Oh shit. Looked like telepathy wasn't his thing. They all heard who he'd like to sleep with.

The pack leader smiled. "That can be arranged."

Excuse me?

"Huh?" Wasn't he full of intelligent remarks tonight?

The pack leader tucked a strand of hair behind her ear. "You," she pointed at Tom, "can mate with her," the finger turned to Vonda, "and we can let you keep Elizabeth. Of course, that's dependent on the bitch there," the finger returned to Vonda, "joining our pack. You have five minutes to decide."

With that declaration, she marched to the other side of the clearing, the pack following. Tom felt the wolves' eyes on him, staring, watching, daring him to make a run for it. If he hadn't seen one of the creatures change before his eyes, he'd think it was all a nightmare from the blow to the head.

But small things in his life, little things he had stuck in the back of his mind over the years, whispered to him, made him know that what the alpha said was true. Werewolves existed and he carried their genetics.

Made him wonder what other secrets Mom had neglected to mention.

"Daddy, if I'm a wolf and they wanted me to join them, why didn't they just ask?" Elizabeth's amber eyes turned toward him, her head resting on his arm.

"Um..."

Because their momma never taught them any manners. I swear, thinking there's nothing wrong with kidnapping little girls, these folks are nuts.

****

But she'd still like to get to know them. And with the mating heat upon her, sleeping with Tom sounded like a wonderful idea. Best idea she'd heard all night.

Of course, she'd have to wait until morning when her human body returned to engage in any of the fun.

Permanent, slid across her mind. Yeah, it would be a permanent type of thing. Would she be able to handle permanence? To move in with Tom? Staying with him when the mating heat vanished?

At least he wouldn't call her a dog.

And he was way ahead of her ex on the attractive scale, the nice scale and the family man scale. All in all she wouldn't mind a bit of horizontal time.

"I'm sorry to drag you into this."

Vonda gave Tom a wolfish shrug, wishing she had her human features so he could read on her face how much she wanted him. Not all of the desire came from the mating heat. Sure, her core pulsed and she wanted nothing more than his staff thrusting into her, filling her, but a part of the desire throbbing in her veins was for Tom. Just Tom.

Something within him spoke to her on a base level.

And she wanted that in a permanent way.

You didn't exactly drag me, you know. I saw them taking her first.

Tom nodded and swallowed, his hand stroking Elizabeth's back, his eyes refusing to meet Vonda's.

A shaky hand shoved through his hair. "Are you willing?"

He spoke the words to the trees, but turned to face her before the sound died.

She didn't hesitate. If he was willing to have her,

knowing she turned furry once a month, she would take him. And she got a hot body in the bargain.

Yep. If you don't mind me looking like this monthly.

He shook his head, opening his mouth to speak, but the alpha chose that moment to return.

"So, what's the decision?"

"She'll move in with me. And you won't be taking my daughter," Tom growled the last words.

Damn, if that wasn't the sexiest thing Vonda had heard.

The alpha nodded. "That is acceptable. We will check on you monthly to see how Elizabeth is." Her eyes moved to Vonda. "And to see if you have questions about us. You need a pack."

Thank you. I would like that.

"Now since you've decided to mate, we will need to make sure you consummate the relationship."

"And just how do you suggest you do that?" Tom's lips pulled back, exposing his teeth.

"I'll follow you back to your house and ensure the mating is consummated. I'll return later to talk more to Vonda about the pack. Are you ready to go?"

Vonda exchanged a glance with Tom. PL was going to watch them? Eww. She didn't get into starring on sex tapes. Talk about performance anxiety.

Elizabeth lifted her head from Tom's shoulder. "Hey, Dad, what's consummated mean?"

Chapter 6

Vonda touched the silver picture frame containing a photo of a black-haired woman in a white, strapless wedding dress and a younger looking Tom. Husband and wife. Until death do us part.

They'd looked so happy, so in love. How could Vonda hope to achieve that with Tom?

First things first. They needed to consummate this agreement, something Tom looked rather hesitant to do. He paced the room, running fingers through his short hair until it stood like captured soldiers, nervous and trembling.

"Elizabeth will be okay. She'll sleep for awhile. Margie put her under and promised she'd stay asleep." The alpha, Margie, had claimed she had the ability to make Elizabeth catch eight hours of zzzs, and set about proving it with a wave of her hand.

Tom stopped his pacing and stared at her. "I should be up there with her, not down here with you." He ran his hand through his hair again, making matters up top worse. "Dammit, that didn't come out right."

"I know what you mean." And she did. Tom should be with his daughter, not trying to have sex with Vonda.

Although sex sounded great at the moment. And how screwed up was that? Mating heat was a bitch.

"Did it hurt?" Tom gestured at her.

Vonda looked down her body from Tom's t-shirt

around her torso to his sweat pants on her legs and wondered what the hell he was talking about.

"Did what hurt?" Having his shirt rub against her sensitive nipples or his pants rest against her already wet core? Somehow she didn't think that was what he wanted to know.

"The change back."

Oh, yeah. That. "Well, it wasn't the best feeling I've ever had." The only thing she could imagine worse would be having her tonsils ripped out through her nose. "But it doesn't seem to have any lingering effects. I didn't realize changing back to a human while the moon was still out was even possible."

Margie was one powerful bitch. Holding her hand toward Vonda, she had forced Vonda's wolf back to its hiding place, bringing out the human half to writhe in agony on the cold linoleum floor of Tom's kitchen. For the first time since she hit puberty, Vonda saw the moon out of her human eyes.

It was worth every bit of pain.

"Maybe she'll show me how to do that. She's going to teach me what it means to be a pack member." Vonda couldn't wait. After all these years alone, she would learn what it meant to be a werewolf. There had to be more to it than getting furry once a month.

"That's good. That's real good." More with the hand through the hair routine. "I need to go check on Elizabeth."

Tom headed for the door, but Vonda beat him to it.

"You can't go anywhere until we, um, until we mate."

Her hand on his arm sparked heat, a tangible arc crossing the air to Tom, stilling him. He took a deep breath, turning to face Vonda. His green eyes smoked with desire, firing the blood in her veins, whipping it into a frenzy being with her ex had never produced.

It was callous of her to want sex after all that had happened tonight, knowing a ten-year-old frightened girl lay upstairs. But with the mating heat firing her blood, she couldn't help it. All she wanted was Tom. His arms around her, his body pressed to her, his thick staff inside her.

Her imagination kicked into overdrive as she pictured him pumping into her, in and out, his big body slamming into her over and over again. She felt wetness between her legs as her core wept, wanting him in her, needing him to complete her.

His nostrils flared. "You smell good," he said, his voice a low growl that distorted the words.

She didn't think she could get wetter, but that growling thing sent her core into overdrive.

Holding his gaze, she started working the buttons on his shirt. His breath sawed in and out of his lungs as her hands crept down his torso. Once the shirt was unbuttoned, she pushed the sleeves down his arms, dropping it onto the floor. She ran her hands up his arms, feeling the muscles tense at her touch. Damn, but the man was strong. She loved the feel of his pecs under her palms, the way the springy hair dusted his chest.

She needed her skin against his. Now.

Working quickly, Vonda yanked her shirt over her head and smiled at a transfixed Tom. Once she dropped the shirt onto the ground, he snapped out of his trance.

His hands shoved her pants over her hips and Vonda kicked them off. A wave of embarrassment passed through her. What if he didn't like the way she looked? Her sexual experiences were limited to fumbles in the dark and a man who called her a dog.

If that growl meant anything, she shouldn't have worried. Tom brushed a hand over her collarbone, across her breasts, down her stomach to her core, the feather-light touch scorching like fire.

"You're beautiful."

Vonda felt her muscles relax at his words.

"You're pretty good looking yourself."

He bent his head, his lips pressing against hers. The tip of his tongue traced the crease between her lips and she opened for him, letting the strokes of his tongue against hers carry her into that place where nothing mattered but the two of them.

Tom held her head with one hand, while his other teased her nipple into a hard point. Vonda stopped thinking, her body pure instinct, wanting him, needing him in her. She fumbled with the button on his Levi's, while his fingers flicked against her nipple. A moan escaped her and she finally freed the darn button, which allowed her to yank the zipper down. She shoved the jeans over his hips then pulled the waistband of his tighty-whities out and over his staff, freeing him for her feeling pleasure.

Vonda ran her hand up the length of him, loving the velvety skin, the thick head, the swollen sac. Damn, but he was huge. She'd be sore tomorrow.

She could hardly wait.

Tom moaned in her mouth as she stroked up the thick length. His thumb rubbed against her swollen nipple as his other hand stroked from her waist to her hip, each pass drawing closer to the place between her legs that ached for him.

He kissed her until her surroundings dimmed, until the only thing that mattered was his lips on hers, his skin against hers, the feel of his staff in her hand as she drew it through her grasp. She circled the broad head, once, twice, feeling wetness seep out of the slit. Rubbing the moisture into his skin, she continued her lazy strokes, up and down, up and circled around, while Tom's hand moved closer to her mound.

He touched her core, his fingers sliding in the wetness he found there. She felt his staff kick in her hand, spurts of cum coating her stomach.

"Shit!" Tom exploded as his hips bucked against her hand, while she milked him dry.

Well, that didn't take long. What about her?

He dropped his head to her shoulder, breathing deeply. "I'm so sorry. It's been awhile since I've...yeah." He tried to take a step and tripped over his jeans, falling into her. "God, I'm sorry. I'm so sorry. This just isn't going to work. Not now anyway. I just..." He ran his hand through his hair.

Vonda blinked. "But what about Margie?"

"Fuck. I don't know."

Vonda looked down and saw cum running down her stomach. She wiped it off, smearing onto her core and the insides of her legs.

"Hey, Margie! It's finished!"

Hopefully the alpha would smell him on her and leave before this night got any worse.

Vonda heard Margie on the other side of the door, breathing deeply.

"Ah, good. The mating is complete. Is Tom...okay?"

"Yeah, I'm good." His hand did another run

through the hair.

"Oh. Well, then. That's great. Great." Why did she sound so disappointed? "I'll let myself out and leave you two lovebirds alone. I'll be back tomorrow afternoon to talk to Vonda."

Vonda and Tom listened as Margie's steps echoed down the hall, the sound of the front door shutting propelling Tom into action.

"God, I'm sorry." He reached for his underwear and jeans, drawing them up in one motion while he talked. "We can...yeah...maybe later, right? I'm going upstairs with Elizabeth. You can have the bed in here."

He yanked his shirt off the floor and closed the door behind him, never once looking her in the eye.

What was it with her and men? She slid one finger inside her while circling her clit with another. Two strokes later and her hips bucked, the orgasm rippling through her. Her body relieved, she wished she could say the same about her heart.

She walked into the bathroom and started cleaning herself with a wet washcloth. How would she face Tom tomorrow? She understood his need to be with his daughter and it was just plain weird to even try to have sex under the circumstances, but still. He could have stuck around long enough get her off too.

Although that wasn't fair, was it? Yes, yes it was. Even if he was embarrassed. Everyone knows men can't always control those things. Vonda pitched the washcloth onto the rim of the bathtub. Still. The mating heat hadn't abated. She could do with a dose of Tom right about now.

But she knew getting him back into the bedroom would be a challenge.

Good thing she loved challenges. She had what was left of the night and all day tomorrow to come up with a plan. Vonda smiled. Yep, Tom would soon discover werewolves didn't give up so easily.

Chapter 7

Tom walked in the back door, leaned against the wall and pulled his muddy boots off. He heard the female voices like a squabble of geese, pecking around the kitchen. Vonda's laughter rang out and then the squabble dropped to a manageable volume.

Shit. He'd managed to avoid Vonda all day. What did you say to a woman when you came all over her and then left the room? Thanks? And what an ass he was, didn't even bother to see to her pleasure.

The only good thing that came of it was he knew his dick still worked in front of a woman.

Now he had to face Vonda and how embarrassing was that. Maybe he could sneak up the back stairs.

"Daddy!" Elizabeth ran around the corner, smack into him, her skinny arms surrounding his waist with a squeeze.

Or maybe he couldn't sneak anywhere.

"Is that you, Tom?" Vonda called.

Yep, not sneaking anywhere. Time to face her. He was a big boy, really. Yep, yep.

"Come on, Daddy. Margie's been telling us about the pack." Elizabeth tugged his hand, drawing him into the kitchen.

Within a few hours, Margie had gone from Elizabeth's worst enemy to her best friend. And wasn't that a good thing. Made things easier on him too.

Margie and Vonda sat at the kitchen table, tea cups in front of them. An extra cup sat in front of an empty chair. Elizabeth slid into the empty and took a sip out of her cup.

"Want some tea, Dad?"

"No, sweetie, I'm good. Just going to change out of these clothes, then I'll come back and fix dinner, okay?" He rubbed his hand over her head, chuckling as she ducked and squeaked, "Daddy!"

He walked out of the room toward his bedroom, feeling Vonda's eyes on him. *Way to continue to avoid her, Tom.*

He had to face her eventually, no getting around it. She would be living here now. Taking Anita's place. Tom grabbed onto the dresser, steadying himself. Not only did he have to deal with his little failure in the bedroom last night, but now he realized he needed to come to grips with Vonda, for all intents and purposes, being his wife.

Anita looked out at him from the photo taken the day of their wedding, her eyes glistening with love. Some of the last coherent words she'd spoken to him asked him to find someone else, someone to keep him warm at night. She was gone, had been gone for four years, her death releasing him from his wedding vows, so why did he feel like being with Vonda was cheating?

It wasn't. Definitely wasn't cheating.

Layla walked into the room, her nails tapping a rhythm on the wood floor as she made her way to the rug under the bed. She huffed as she plopped down on the rug, her expression one of extreme exasperation.

Tom took a breath and shut the door. "What's the matter, old girl? You think I need to move on?"

As usual she remained silent. Like a dog can talk. Wolves on the other hand...

He ran his hand through his hair. In the last twenty-four hours he'd had his daughter kidnapped and returned, been given a mate who turned furry once a month and discovered he was half werewolf. If he had any more revelations, he'd need to change his name to John the Baptist.

Tonight he needed to talk to Vonda. He would, once Elizabeth went to bed, which gave him even more time to avoid the unavoidable. Yee-haw.

Tom dropped his shirt and pants into the clothes hamper and shrugged on a t-shirt and jeans. Layla remained curled on the rug by the bed, waiting for him to dress. Tom looked from his dog to the bed, the bed where he spent many a fine night with Anita, the bed where he would spend many more nights with Vonda.

All day he'd thought about Vonda, what he would say, more importantly, what he would do to her body. He felt his erection grow at the thought of Vonda, her brown wavy hair, her amber eyes, her small hand as it grasped his dick, drawing out his pleasure.

Damn. He couldn't go out to the kitchen looking like he'd stuffed a potato down his pants. Think, think. Yeah, fixing fences, nothing sexy about that one. Or he could look at the picture of his wife on their wedding day. Yep, that one did the trick.

Tom ran his hand through his hair.

"I hope you don't mind," he whispered to the picture. "I mean, you asked me to find someone and I did. More like she found me, but whatever, I'm going to take her tonight. Elizabeth will have the mother she needs and I, well, I like her too. I hope that doesn't bother you."

Was it his imagination or did the picture shake its head? He definitely needed some water; he must have been out in the sun too long.

"I love you, Anita, I'll always love you. But Vonda's here with me now and I need her. I hope you understand and that you aren't mad. What the hell am I saying? You're not even here. I'm talking to ghosts again."

The picture frame felt cold in his hand. With a last look at the picture, he placed it in the dresser drawer. She was dead. Four years now. Time he got on with his life.

The woman he wanted now sat at his kitchen table and there was no room for ghosts.

****

Vonda watched as Tom walked back into the kitchen and started to pull things out of the freezer. Pots and pans flopped on the stove in a rush of movement. Nothing more sexy than a man who can cook. Especially a man who rocked a pair of faded Levi's.

She took a sip of the now-cool tea and openly ogled Tom's butt. Damn, but the man was hot. She needed to stop ogling especially since Elizabeth sat next to her. Needed to set a good example, since she was going to be the girl's step-mom.

The tea went down the wrong way. Margie slapped Vonda on the back as Vonda wheezed and hacked.

"You okay?" Tom stopped chopping vegetables and looked at Vonda.

She nodded, whacking herself on the chest. Apparently drinking while thinking of impending motherhood, even if it was motherhood by step instead of birth, should be avoided. At least Elizabeth seemed to like her and the feeling was returned. Of course she doubted Elizabeth realized Vonda was the new mother figure in her life.

"Well, I should run. Things to do on the full moon. Will you be running with us tonight, Vonda?" Margie stood and hung her purse over her shoulder.

Vonda coughed one more time. "I'll probably just stick around here, but will look for ya'll."

"Well, if we don't see you this time, there's always next month."

"True. Hope you have a good run."

"Same to you. Bye, Elizabeth. Bye, Tom."

"Bye." Tom raised a hand and went back to seasoning meat.

Margie showed herself to the door, while Vonda picked up the used tea cups and placed them in the dishwasher.

"What did you do today, Elizabeth?" Tom asked.

Elizabeth leaned on the counter, watching Tom work.

"Vonda took me to her place to grab some clothes because she said she's crashing here for awhile. Then we went to eat at the deli. Margie was here when we got back and she talked to us for the rest of the afternoon. What did you do?"

Vonda listened to them talk as she set the table. It was not her imagination Tom ignored her. On another day that would bother her, but today she didn't mind. Margie had explained some things, some very interesting things, when Elizabeth offered to play the piano for them. Once she heard what Margie had to say about the matter, she could hardly wait to see if the alpha was correct.

And to do that, she needed to convince Tom to sleep with her before the sun went down.

Time was running out and she still hadn't discovered how to get Elizabeth to leave them alone. But she'd think of something. She needed Tom and if Margie was correct, he needed her as his lover more than he knew. And as the moon would rise in a couple of hours, she didn't have long to convince him of it.

Good thing she liked challenges.

Chapter 8

"Elizabeth, why don't you go practice the piano? Vonda and I have some things to discuss and we don't need an interruption, okay?" Tom looked at Elizabeth as they cleaned up the kitchen after dinner.

"But I practiced this afternoon for Margie."

"Is there something you could do in your room?"

"So like, you're kicking me out of the first floor?"

"Pretty much."

Elizabeth shook her head. "Adults. You guys are just weird. Fine, I'll go read a book, okay?"

Tom patted her back. "Thanks honey."

"And I'm going now. You can finish up the kitchen."

"Hey..."

"You asked for that one," Vonda said as Elizabeth huffed up the stairs. "Not like I'm complaining. You just solved my big dilemma of the day."

She leaned against the counter, hand outstretched for a plate to put in the dishwasher.

"Glad to be of service." He handed her a plate to put in the rack. "Now if I could just solve one of mine. Something's been eating my herd each month. Only one or two head, but..."

Vonda looked at the ceiling. That corner might need a broom. Looked like a cobweb hung there. She glanced back at Tom. That white-knuckled grip he had on the dishrag was bound to hurt.

"You? You've been eating my herd?"

Busted.

She shrugged. "They were there."

"So are deer. And they need thinning."

"But they aren't steak tartare. I love steak tartare."

"That herd's my living!" He threw the dishrag into the sink.

"It was only one."

"Yeah, one a month."

Vonda looked at his feet. Being busted was so not her idea of fun. "I didn't mean to take all of them from you. I'm new to the area and wanted to eat. I thought it was from different ranchers."

Tom sighed and picked up the dishrag, which he shook at her, wet sprinkles emphasizing his words. "Promise me you won't do it again."

"Okay, I'll try. But I can't a hundred percent promise. You have no idea how good they taste off the bone."

"Try. Please. Go eat deer. I'll buy you steak tartare in a nice restaurant. Please." His green eyes beseeched her.

Who could resist those peepers? "I'll try really hard."

****

Tom stared at Vonda. Unbelievable. *She* caused the thinning of his herd. Even so, even though he should still be pissed at her, he found her attractive. Her amber eyes gleamed with mischief and desire. Despite his failure last night, she wanted him. And he wanted her. More than he wanted his herd to live, he wanted this woman. What was it about Vonda that turned him on, that made him forget his anger?

"It's my sexy good looks." She smiled at him, wiggling her eyebrows.

"Are you reading my mind again?"

"You're broadcasting again. It's hard not to know what you're thinking."

Tom took a breath, wondering if she'd know the answer to one question that plagued him all day. Or plagued him in those small moments when he wasn't contemplating what to do to Vonda's body.

"Did Margie say why, if I'm a genetically defective werewolf, I have telepathic abilities? Among other things."

"What other things?" Vonda stuck another plate in the rack.

"Did she or didn't she?"

"Maybe. What other things?"

"Are you always this stubborn?"

Vonda grinned. "On occasion."

Tom snorted. "Uh-huh. I'll go first. Sometimes I know what's going to happen before it happens. Now it's your turn."

"She might have mentioned something."

"Hey, no fair. I told you, the least you can do is return the favor."

"I will. But there are other things that have been on my mind all day concerning you and talking isn't it." Vonda raised her eyes to his, her amber irises glowing.

Ditto for him. So far this conversation was better than he thought it would be. "Yeah? Like what?" He couldn't help the grin that curled his lips.

She lightly slapped him on the upper arm. "Like what?"

Tom caught her wrist and pulled her toward him. "I can do better than last night if you'd like to try it."

Her hands slid up his chest, winding around the nape of his neck. "You have really good ideas tonight, mister."

"Glad you like them."

Warm lips touched his and the same spark he felt yesterday when he shook her hand shot through him. Heat circulated through his body, his heart thumping a frantic beat. Muscles tightened as if he prepared for a race instead of a horizontal bed session. The scent of Vonda's skin pushed his desire to a new level, thickening his erection. If the damn thing got any bigger, it would unzip his pants on its own. Not like he was complaining, at least all parts were a go.

Vonda's body pressed against his as he deepened the kiss, stroking his tongue against hers. With one foot, he closed the dishwasher door.

"Why don't we go in the bedroom?" Tom whispered in Vonda's ear.

She shivered. "What's wrong with the kitchen?"

"Elizabeth might not stay put."

"Oh, yeah. Bedroom it is."

She started walking in the direction of the bedroom, but Tom reached for her hand, turning her to face him. Lowering his head, he kissed her, not wanting to lose contact with her body even for the short distance to the bedroom. Vonda let out a little squeak when he wrapped his arms around her waist and lifted her off her feet.

Despite what studies showed about men, he could do two things at once, kissing and walking while holding Vonda. And with his erection straining against his zipper after four years of inactivity, he was so the man.

Despite his poor performance last night and the fact Vonda would be the only woman since his wife died who he slept with, he felt an amazing lack of nerves. Being with Vonda felt right, as if his entire life happened to lead him to her.

The bedroom door shut with a resounding click when he nudged it with his foot, closing him in with his fate.

****

Vonda moaned as Tom's tongue swept against hers. His kisses made her legs weak. Thank goodness his arms remained around her waist, keeping her from falling. She tilted her head back as he kissed down her neck, nipping gently at her shoulder. The fire that shot through her veins burned hotter than anything she felt before. Something about being around Tom made the mating heat stronger, and yet his touch calmed her. As if curling up next to him would make everything in her life okay.

His mouth burned a trail of kisses from her shoulder across her skin to where her tank top began. When his arms loosened around her waist, she clutched at his shirt to remain on her feet. Tom slid his hands under her tank top, pulled it over her head and dropped it on the floor in one movement. He traced a finger around the lace cups of her bra.

"Sexy." He winked at her and sprang the back clasp free.

Before he could remove it, Vonda locked gazes with Tom and slowly lowered the straps down her arms, teasing him with small glimpses of her nipples, while she held the bra cups in place with one hand. His gaze left hers, fixating on her chest. Slowly, ever so slowly, she lowered the cups, the lace rasping against her sensitive nubs.

Tom licked his lips, glanced at her face and dropped his mouth to one nipple. With his tongue, he circled the bud, driving her crazy before finally drawing it into his mouth. Vonda sighed as she ran her hands through his hair, holding him against her. The man had talented lips, fingers, tongue. Wonder if all parts of him were equally good?

Probably.

His mouth moved to her other nipple, while one warm finger circled the nub he had sucked, the contrast of warm finger and cold air causing chill bumps to form across her skin. She felt desire rushing through her blood, heating her, her core growing wet for him, because of him.

She wanted the feel of his skin against her. Needed it. Needed him. His shirt had to go. Now. Even if it meant breaking the connection of his mouth against her breast.

Vonda yanked his t-shirt out of his pants, shoving it up until it caught on his arms. Drat it.

"Eager, eh?" Tom grinned at her, male satisfaction gleaming in his eyes.

"You have no idea." Vonda managed to yank the offending t-shirt over his head and deposited it on the pile of clothes littering the floor. About time some article of his clothing joined the pile.

"I like you like this. Wanting me."

She smiled at him, pulling him close for a kiss. The mating heat might rule her hormones and cause her to need sex, but it didn't make her long for his touch. The longing was all Tom's doing. She had never wanted a man like this before.

She trailed kisses to his ear, while his fingers played with her nipples, circling, pinching.

"God, Tom, you make me want you. Now."

"Hmm. That's what I like to hear. But it's denied." He flicked a fingernail across her nipple, eliciting a groan from her. "You have to wait. I have a lot to make up for."

"Mmm. I like that idea. Unfortunately the sun sets soon, so unless you want a furry wolf in your bed, you need to get a move on."

"You have a point."

She reached for the button of his jeans. "Let's make you more comfortable."

His hands ran down her ribs, over her waist, stopping on the waistband of her low rise jeans. "Ditto for you."

And then he kissed her and all thoughts except for getting that damn button undone left her mind. In a rush of hands, sweep of arms and some fancy footwork, they both managed to remove each other's jeans and underwear.

Vonda felt the bed hit the back of her knees and she tumbled onto the patchwork quilt covering the mattress. Tom's weight fell on top of her, a delicious blanket of warmth and comfort.

She wrapped her legs around his waist as his hips rolled against hers, his staff rasping against her sensitive clit. He pulled back and thrust forward, teasing her, making her groan.

The fire built in her veins, centered in her core, as

he continued teasing her clit, thrusting, pulling back, until she started convulsing. One big hand touched her mound.

"Not yet. I want to be in you when you come."

"Well then, hurry it up!"

Tom chuckled. Using his hand, he guided that huge erection to her entrance. Locking gazes with her, he thrust into her core, sinking to the hilt. Vonda gasped as he filled her. For sure she'd be sore tomorrow. His thumb stroked her cheek, concern in his eyes.

"You okay? I'm a little big."

"A little? Feels good. Would feel better if you'd move." She tightened her legs, pushing his hips into hers.

Tom smiled and did as she wanted, pulling back and slamming into her, over and over again until she tightened around him, crying out. Two thrusts later and he joined her, spilling into her spasming channel.

Dropping her legs from his waist, Vonda ran a hand through his hair and kissed his cheek. He raised himself onto his arms and tucked a strand of her hair behind her ear. A wrinkle appeared between his eyes, the anxiety bleeding into his gaze.

She smiled. "That was great. We'll have to do a repeat later. Like when I'm human again." Maybe Margie didn't know what she was talking about. Everything looked to be normal. Oh, well. It had been an interesting theory.

The anxiety in his eyes vanished, replaced by joy. "We have a deal." He pulled out, the absence of his weight leaving her feeling abandoned. Odd, that.

Since Margie was so obviously incorrect, Vonda needed to clean up and mentally prep for the bone-wrenching pain of the change. After all these years of changing, she knew when the sun was about to set, when the magic of the change would overcome her, turning her into a wolf. Shouldn't be much longer now.

Vonda made it halfway to the bathroom when she heard Tom cry out. She whirled around to see him kneeling by the bed, one hand bracing himself against it. Pain-filled eyes turned to her.

"God, Vonda, what's happening?" His voice broke, the ending of the last word coming out in a growl.

The skin on his back rippled and the oddest thought crossed her mind. The only time she'd seen another person change was when Margie forced it from Big G. And that happened so quickly, Vonda hadn't processed it. But this, this she processed. Did she look like that when she changed?

"Congrats. You're not genetically deficient after all."

He panted, gritting his teeth against the pain. "Huh?"

"You're changing." She knelt beside him, touching his shoulder. "Margie said it can happen if a half-breed who hasn't changed has sex with a full-breed. That's why she stuck around last night, to see if you'd changed. Guess she'll be surprised tomorrow. Shh, just relax, let it flow over you, don't fight it." Naturally, he fought it. She had too, all those years ago. Until she realized changing was much easier if she relaxed and let it happen.

"It hurts."

She ran her hand through his hair wanting to take the pain from him. "I know. It will go away once the change is complete."

Tom opened his mouth as if to speak, but before he could, she saw the beast inside him win the fight. His face changed, growing longer, growing fur. He yelled, the sound turning into a howl as he changed. Fur rippled across his skin, brown fur tipped in black as if he were a calligraphy brush dipped in ink. His arms turned into legs and he collapsed on the floor.

Damn. Does it hurt like that all the time? His voice sounded in her head.

"Not quite that bad, but it's still painful."

Vonda felt the sun drop below the horizon, the magic in her veins pulling her beast out. Her skin rippled like Tom's had, flowing into fur as she dropped to all fours, shaking the pain from her muscles. Unlike Tom she had grown used to the pain, or as used to pain as one could get.

Footsteps sounded at a fast pace, followed by a pounding on their door.

"Daddy! Are you okay? I heard yelling. Daddy?"

Elizabeth opened the door and burst into the room, coming to a halt as she stared at the two wolves. Fear crossed her eyes, but she held her ground.

"Vonda? Daddy?"

Don't be scared, honey. I seem to have changed.

It's okay, Elizabeth. Your Dad changed like me, Vonda said at the same time.

Elizabeth's eyes darted from one wolf to the other. "Oh, my gosh. Daddy changed into a wolf. How wicked cool!"

How wicked painful, Tom muttered.

Elizabeth didn't hear him. She ran over to him and threw her arms around his neck. Tom licked her face.

"Does this mean Margie isn't going to try to take

me again? I like her, but I don't want to live with her."

No, sweetie, that's why Vonda's going to live with us, Margie isn't going to take you from me.

"But you're a wolf now."

I am, but Vonda is going to stay here and show us how to be wolves. Someone has to and I'd rather it be Vonda than Margie, wouldn't you?

Elizabeth looked at Vonda and then back and Tom. Vonda kept her mouth shut. She was staying, no way was she letting Tom go, but Tom needed to explain things to Elizabeth. If it wasn't for Tom's change, she'd have left the two of them alone to talk things out.

"Yeah, I like Vonda. She can stay."

Vonda gave her a toothy grin. Score, she was in with the kid. For now.

Tom, I'm going to run. You want to come with me? I promise I won't eat your cattle.

"She was eating on the herd?" Elizabeth's brows shook hands with her hairline.

They were tasty, but your dad made me promise not to eat his herd. One of these days you'll understand the taste.

"Eww. I don't think so."

Honey, I'm going to go out with Vonda. You stay here. Keep the doors and windows shut and locked and we'll be back by morning. We'll be around the area if you need us. Okay?

Elizabeth shrugged. "No one's coming after me again, right?"

Right, honey. Will you be okay?

"Sure. Soon I can go out with you, too. Cool. I'm going to go read. Maybe I'll stay up all night reading since you won't be around to tell me otherwise."

Hey, now...

Elizabeth jumped up, kissed Tom's head and darted out the door.

She doesn't listen to me, Tom sighed.

Yeah? Get used to it. They tend to do that.

Are you happy with this? His paw gestured to her and back to him.

This?

Me. Like this. Or not like this. I mean, are you happy with this decision? It was forced on you and I appreciate you offering to stay with us so I could keep Elizabeth, but I want you to be happy with the decision.

Rambling. He was rambling. Vonda smiled to herself. If a man rambles, well, that means he cares. And Tom caring enough about her to ramble made her heart sing.

I'm very happy. Ever since I met you, since I shook your hand, I've wanted you. And not just the sex thing. It's you. I've never felt about a man like I do you. I'm more than happy with this arrangement.

He walked over to her and licked her face.

It's a little hard to do what I want in this body. But once the sun comes up, don't run off. He waggled the hair sticking out above his eyes.

She licked him back. *Don't worry, I won't. Are you ready for the hunt?*

As long as you're with me, I'm ready for anything.

Anything? Her eyebrows waggled back at him.

Anything with you. Forever and always.

With Tom at her side and in her heart, the loneliness she experienced her entire life vanished, leaving only peace.

Wolf Mates

by

Karilyn Bentley

Dedication

To Lill:
This one's for you.
If not for our conversation that day at Starbucks, there
would be no vegetarian werewolf.

Chapter One

A vegetarian werewolf was an oxymoron on a number of different levels. Could she even call herself a vegetarian if she took down that grazing deer? The usual monthly guilt slapped her like a twig on the snout. Her wolf instincts insisted she eat the deer. After all, she was a wolf and wolves preyed on deer, right? *Right.*

Everyone knew wolves needed meat. Just because her two-legged self thought otherwise didn't mean her four-legged one couldn't eat it.

So much for the guilt. If she crammed it under a dark corner of her being, it couldn't bother her, now could it?

Nope, no bothering allowed from that dark place. At least not until after dinner. With her guilt temporarily buried, Margie focused on the grazing deer. Her pack spread out, slinking through the trees to surround the herd. Tails wagging, they paused, waiting for her signal.

Margie scented the air, drawing the ripeness of earth and animals deep into her lungs. Upwind of the deer, she watched their ears twitch, their muscles tighten as they looked around the stream where they stopped to drink. The poor beasts knew they were dinner, they just didn't know the time or location.

Her lip curled. *A couple of minutes and here, my yummies.*

Margie looked at her pack—the males and females and a few of their young on their first hunt—that belonged to her. As alpha, it was her responsibility to care for them, to provide food. Good thing elk and deer were plentiful. She picked out two for dinner.

The young male on the right with the cut on its leg and the old one on the left. Is everyone in position?

Ready, alpha! Voices chorused through her mind.

Go!

As one, they sprang forward, legs churning, a few of the younger wolves on their first hunt yipping with obvious joy. The deer ran, crashing through the underbrush, releasing scents of grass and dry wood. Hunting was a thrill ride, a high-paced, adrenaline charged run. Her blood thrummed through her veins, her breath sawed in and out, as she jumped over logs, twigs catching in her fur.

The young male fell first, neck snapped from a pack enforcer's leap. Within seconds, the older stag joined the first, legs thrashing against the ground in a futile attempt to ward off death, before it too lay still. The rest of the herd continued their frantic flight, leaving their fallen comrades as the main meal on werewolf-night-at-the-ranch.

Margie trotted toward the young male. Alphas ate first so she might as well get dinner started. Guilt came back with a vengeance, hammering in her mind, telling her to run away, to avoid eating meat. Once again she ignored it. It was wrong, the wolf was right, dinner was served.

Take that, guilt.

Her teeth tore into the belly of the deer, pulling out the entrails. The best part, in her opinion. Not everyone agreed, as a good deal of her pack started in on the rumps. To each his own.

When she finished eating, she lay down in a bed of leaves and watched her pack. Wolves, including those of the were variety, finished off the entire deer, leaving very little behind. Some of her pack had eaten the meat away from the leg, and deer bones glistened bright white under the full moon. What she wouldn't give for one of those bones. She loved the marrow.

Yet another thing for the guilt to notice.

What had possessed her to become a vegetarian? She remembered the day she had informed her parents of her decision. At seventeen, she thought she knew everything. And that everything meant she knew, just knew, eliminating meat from her diet was for the best. And it might very well have been if she had been fully human and didn't turn furry once a month. As it was, her parents laughed so hard it made her determined to stick to her decision. No matter what happened.

Stupid teenager stubbornness.

Even in human form, staying vegetarian was hard. If she saw raw meat, she salivated no matter which form she was in. Her pack didn't understand her odd choice, not that it mattered. All that mattered was they followed her, and follow her they did, some more eagerly than others.

Not many packs had only an alpha female. Most packs had either an alpha pair or a male alpha. So she was an oddity all around.

Plenty of lone wolves visited or joined her pack, most just to get a glimpse of how she ran things. They returned home once they realized no difference existed between her and a male alpha. Except for her lack of a huge-ass pair of balls dangling between her legs. At first it bothered her, the curiosity and stares, but now she was so used to it she barely paid attention.

The new members were another matter.

Take Landa, for instance. Landa's name barely finished flitting across her mind when the white wolf grabbed a bone and trotted to Margie, ears back, tail down.

Now that was freaky. Maybe Landa read minds. When Landa came within five feet of Margie, she dropped into a prone position and crawled, bone in mouth, to Margie's feet, where she dropped the bone.

I thought you might want this, alpha.

Thank you, Landa. That was very thoughtful and insightful of you.

Margie swore if Landa had been in human form she would have blushed.

Thank you, alpha.

Landa slunk back several feet before walking back to the pack and her dinner.

That was ... odd. But no use wasting the bone.

Margie grabbed the bone, gnawing on it as she watched Landa. Long white fur, tipped with black on the ends, covered what appeared to be an omega.

And yet, some whisper of strength laced the female's spirit and shone through her cornflower blue eyes. Margie took a cue from the military and ran a don't-ask-don't-tell pack. A policy she'd been close to breaking in Landa's case. Even after four months of living among her pack, Landa's neck still bore a bare spot in her fur. In her human body, the area formed a mass of red scar tissue encircling her neck. It looked like the descriptions she'd read of scars left by slave bands. But what kind of person could put slave bands on a werewolf?

Even the most omega of her pack would fight and kill a human that tried to put them in chains, which left a werewolf as the culprit. But what kind of werewolf would put a band on a pack member?

None that she knew of, and as alpha she knew most of the pack leaders in America and some from other countries. Even those she didn't know personally, she had heard of, and no one anywhere had mentioned placing bands on their members.

Yep, she needed to change her policy. It was pretty obvious Landa wasn't going to chat about her former life, so she needed to be a leader and discover the details.

Which was much easier said than carried through.

Given enough time, she was certain Landa would tell all, or at least some. Starting with how that scar got on her neck. Margie crunched the bone. *Ah, bliss.* Bones were heaven on earth, clichéd but true. And they gave her time to think about things. Unfortunately, thinking on things did not bring any answers. And in Landa's case, she needed answers.

Something about the wolf was off. What was it? Two crunches later and she hit the marrow. *Yummy.* Oh, yeah, Landa's odd behavior. Granted, her pack gave her the respect due as alpha, but they didn't grovel around and flinch if she looked sideways at them. So why—

Alpha! Big George, one of her enforcers and the only tattooed wolf she knew, darted through the pack, sliding to a stop before her. As a human, George, or Big G as the pack called him, was six-foot nine-inches of tattooed hardness. As a wolf he was the size of a pony with sinewy muscles covered by gray-and-black fur.

Damn shame he had the IQ of Forest Gump on a bad day. Not that it mattered, he was the best enforcer she'd ever met.

What's the matter, Big G?

Shots! Hunters are closing in.

Bullshit! This is my property. What the hell do they think they're doing trespassing on my property? Margie stood, hackles raised. How dare hunters interrupt her bone-chewing bliss?

They're not on your property, they're right to the east of it.

Whew. She glanced at the discarded bone. *Okay. So what's the problem?*

They have a werewolf in their sights.

What! Why didn't he mention that first? Starting out the conversation with that little tidbit of info would have been nice.

They have a werewolf—

Where?

To the east.

Lead the way.

Two quick shout-outs, one to the pack's remaining five enforcers to follow and the second for the others to stay, and they ran, heading toward the last location of the hunters. Wind rushed across her face, catching her whiskers, bringing with it the scent of gunpowder and sweat.

Damn hunters. Ever since the law relaxed, hunters were allowed to kill wolves even if the wolf hadn't attacked their livestock. As a consequence, wolves were dying and werewolves needed to watch where they turned and where they ran. Her pack ran on her territory, The Flying Fur Dude Ranch, which meant they never ran afoul of hunters.

But judging by the scent of were blood, someone hadn't been so lucky.

A barbed-wire fence stopped their flight, a barrier stretching the perimeter of her property to keep out unwanted guests. Margie pulled up short along with everyone else. Everyone except for Big G, who leapt the fence as if it was only two-feet high. As soon as all four feet landed, he pivoted, teeth gleaming white. Show off.

Climb through it.

Holding down the bottom strand of the fence with her left front foot, she stuck her muzzle and right front foot over the wire, while ducking under the middle strand. She stepped her rear legs over and ta-da, she was through. Nothing like having a human brain in a wolf's body. A full-blooded wolf would never have thought to crawl through the fence.

Once gathered on the other side of the fence, Margie turned to her crew. *Tread lightly. The hunters are still out there. We need to get the were and bring him or her back. Do you understand?*

Yes, alpha.

Taking a deep breath, pulling scent deeply into her lungs, she turned toward the direction where the injured werewolf lay. Her body tingled from the deep inhalation, tingled like she'd heard it would in the presence of an available alpha. How the hell could she have suggested to her enforcers that the injured wolf was female? Had her sniffer lost its scenting ability?

She quickened her pace and the others fell away, disappearing in her single-minded obsession to get to the downed alpha male. No male she had ever encountered caused this type of reaction, a crazed mixture of hormones and heat surging through her blood.

Oh shit. She had a sneaking suspicion she knew what the sudden rush of crazed hormones meant. Just what she needed—a mate.

Although, she had to admit, the grumbling bunch of elders in her pack would be happy. All those, "why-haven't-you-found-a-mate," comments would vanish like ice on a hot day. The only good that came from all those forced meetings with other single alphas is that she found comrades-in-arms, a band of alphas perfectly happy to be single. The difference being that the male alphas weren't being forced to find a mate with the same strong-arm effort her elders took with her. No "the-balance-of-the-pack-is-off," comments for single male alphas. Their elders might think it, but didn't dare say it. Ah, the joys of having a swinging set. If she had been born male, she wouldn't have to accuse her elders of being behind the times.

She might want a mate and a family, but not at the loss of her independence. Male alphas always wanted control and she enjoyed being self-reliant. Besides, despite the grumblings of her elders, her pack prospered. They had money, pack members got along, and the number of new pack members had doubled since she became alpha. Some of that was due to the oddity of a single female alpha, but they did join the pack. What would happen to her pack if she mated a strange male and he took over?

He'd foul it all up. No thank you, she did not want a male all up in her business. She wanted to remain as she was, single.

Unfortunately it looked like fate had other plans.

Drat, drat and double drat. The alpha they rushed toward smelled like her mate.

She was so screwed.

A crack of a branch sounded to her right. She stopped, eyes squinting, nose quivering. Hunters.

Alpha, there're four of them bastards. May I eat one?

Get real, Big G. No.

Dumbass, Jace joined in. *If you eat one, it will only cause more of 'em to come kill off the wolves.*

Oh. Didn't think of that.

As usual. But she loved the big brute. *I'll take care of them. Jace, circle around behind them. Wait for my signal to howl and then run like lightning to the ranch.*

Understood, alpha.

She waited until Jace loped away into the darkness before following the scent of injured werewolf. Leaves crunched under her feet, a permanent carpet of detritus that littered the ground. The scent of blood grew stronger the farther she walked.

"Hey, Joe," one of the hunters yelled, "the blood trail leads this way."

Was it her sensitive ears or were these hunters incompetent? The crash of their boots through the underbrush echoed in her bones. She'd be damned if she let them get to the were before she did.

Sticking nose to the ground, she picked up his blood trail as it led deeper into the woods. The soft padding of feet reassured that her enforcers walked close by, following her. Tree branches groaned, shifting against each other as the wind picked up strength.

Margie sniffed the air, smelling ozone on the breeze.

A storm?

Shit.

A flicker of white fur flashed as branches shifted, allowing a thin stream of moonlight through their leaves. Ah. There was her werewolf. But was he alive?

Sticking her nose into his fur, she inhaled, searching for a breath, a heartbeat, some movement that meant he lived. Blood soaked his fur, but his chest expanded. Not good, but at least he lived.

For now.

"Well, well, there's another one."

Margie's head shot up as a snarl broke across her face. She might not be able to kill those hunters, but nothing said she couldn't mess with their minds. Drawing her magic from its resting place deep inside her, she expanded it through her limbs. Magic thick as summer air before a storm flashed across her skin, danced through her pores, rejoiced at freedom.

Alpha?

She felt Big G's confusion, felt the fear of the other enforcers as they drew closer.

"Shee-it Joe, it's a whole damn pack of them. And what's with that bitch in front?"

She'd show them what's with the bitch. The bitch was pissed. And no one, but no one, messed with the bitch. Especially when said bitch had enough magic flowing through her veins to light up a small town.

Alpha?

No doubt she'd scared her enforcers with her magic display, they never saw her work magic other than the magic used by all alphas. Alpha magic meant she could cause a member of her pack to change at her will, not theirs, or she could will a person into a restful sleep. That kind of magic was inherent within every alpha.

Her kind of magic was one-step away from forbidden.

In some packs, including the one her father ran and she grew up in, it *was* forbidden. That hadn't stopped her from learning it.

She exhaled a sharp breath, letting a visible puff of magic free, and then she blew on the white cloud of air. Expanding outward, the magic grew, becoming a fog, blocking her from the hunters' view.

"Where the hell did that fog come from?"

"Don't know. It wasn't here just a minute ago."

Now, Jace!

Jace howled, the sound slapping against the trees, spinning the hunters around. They might not see her, but she could see them.

"Damn, these woods are full of wolves."

You want to go find the others and leave this one alone. You want to go find the others.

"Let's go get the other one. It's not foggy in that direction."

Nothing like a little suggestion to nudge them on. Who said magic was wrong? One problem down, one to go. The wounded alpha wolf needed to be returned to her pack's infirmary and the sooner the better. But how?

They were in wolf form outside of her property and the wounded wolf was huge. Her gaze darted from the injured alpha and locked on a tattooed wolf the size of a pony. The alpha might be big, but not anywhere near the size of her enforcer.

Big G shook his head. *Tell me you're not thinking what I think you're thinking.*

Margie raised a shoulder and cocked her head in a wolfish shrug. What other choice did she have? *Sorry.*

Chapter Two

Zane woke to arms wrapped around him. Male arms. Male werewolf arms. Adrenaline kicked in, banging through his veins, fueling his anger, all resulting in a great big nothing. What the fuck? Why was he being carried?

He sucked in a breath and a snap-kick of pain shot through his ribs. Oh, shit. Not good. Had he been shot in the side? Where was he?

The last thing he remembered was a loud report ricocheting through the trees. He must have crawled and hidden from the hunters who were chasing him. What an idiot to forget that out here in Montana they hunted wolves like Easter eggs. If he hadn't been a were, he'd likely be dead. Even so, he could die if the bullet lodged in his side wasn't removed before his fast healing ability sealed it in.

He might know what happened to him, but he sure as hell didn't know whose arms surrounded him. A light touch brushed his head, ruffling his fur.

"Shh. You're among your kind. We'll take care of you."

The female voice came from the side and soothed across his pain, a calming balm in a storm. He sucked a breath in and his eyes popped wide. The scent of the female werewolf lodged in his brain, firing his instincts, marking her as his.

Holy shit, he'd found his mate.

And he was too injured to claim her.

Fuck. His eyes rolled and darkness crept toward him, blocking the shadowy outline of the female wolf. *No, no, no.* He would not pass out. Only sissies fainted. But judging by the fact that with his next remembered breath, instead of arms wrapped around him, the soft pad of a mattress cushioned his backside, he concluded he must be a sissy.

Great. He was in the middle of effing Montana, shot, half dead, and in a strange bed. At least the place smelled like werewolf instead of a human hospital, which was one thing in his favor.

Did that mean he'd found what he'd been looking for? Were the rumors right? Or had he been chasing smoke?

And what would Sid do if he found out Zane used Sid's seek-and-find mission to further his own agenda? Maybe Lady Luck would actually be on his side for once and let Sid remain clueless.

Yeah, right. When pigs flew out his ass.

But then, Lady Luck introduced him to his mate— provided he could find her again—so maybe he should be checking for winged pigs.

The hum of a fan turning on followed by a soft breeze crossing his skin had him tilting his head to the sound. Keeping his eyes closed, he took a deep breath through his nose. His human nose. How long had he been unconscious? It must be morning for him to have turned in his unconscious state. The damn torc he wore prevented him from turning at will, which meant he smelled like an alpha, but turned furry like a lesser rank. Sun went down and there was a full moon, he turned into a werewolf; sun came back up and he became human. As an alpha, he should be able to change at will.

Once he got rid of this damn torc, Sid was dead.

The click of a turning doorknob and a squeak of hinges had his lids rolling upward. Light glowed from a lamp sitting on a stand next to the bed, pushing the darkness away from where he lay.

"Well, well, I see our newest addition is awake." Zane squinted at the doorway, at the man standing hidden in shadows. "How are you feeling, pal?" The man stepped into the light, his gaze running from the top of Zane's head to the middle of his chest, all business-like and professional.

Obviously his hosts' vet-doctor.

"My name is Allen Erickson, and I'm the London, Montana pack's vet-doctor."

Good job guessing his visitor's purpose. It seemed his higher brain function still worked. Yay, him. Of course the black bag the man carried was a pretty good clue. Zane pushed up to a sitting position, ignoring the pain in his side.

"I'm Zane Moskos. What happened? Where am I?"

"You got shot, pal. Damn hunters out roaming around killing cousins, thinking they're all big shots. We brought you back here, to the Flying Fur Dude Ranch. You're in our underground infirmary."

"You brought a wolf into a place where humans stay?"

"Are you kidding? We close up shop for three days at the full moon. I take it you aren't from around here?" Allen yanked down the sheet and pulled back the bandage covering Zane's chest.

Zane flinched. "Nope. Not from around here."

"Hmm. Where you from?" Allen peered at Zane's incision.

"How's it look, doc?" Allen could think again if he thought Zane was handing out info about his life.

"You're healing up all nice-like. Had to remove a bullet that nicked a rib but it missed vital organs. You'll have some pain for awhile, but it will go away. Doesn't look like an infection is setting in. How are you feeling?"

Like a train rolled over my chest. "Not too bad."

"Hmm. You don't have to front to me, you know. I can smell your pain." Allen crossed his arms, his stance a muscular six-feet of looming over-confidence.

Zane bristled, his lip curling.

Allen's gaze flitted away and returned to Zane. "You might be an alpha, but I'm a vet-doctor and in this, I'm above you. Now do you want to be in pain for the next several days, or do you want to suck up that attitude and let me help you?"

Zane let loose with a subsonic growl that removed a small bit of confidence off the vet-doctor's face. He wanted to refuse the help, but the reality was, he hated being in pain. Why fight it? Having pride was not the same thing as being stupid.

His lip relaxed and he sank against the pillows. "Fine. Fire away."

Allen picked his bag up off the floor and set it on the bed. Snapping the clasp free, he pawed through the contents. "Ah-ha. Here it is." He pulled a bottle out and shook it in the air, contents rattling inside. "One Vicodin tablet."

Zane held out his hand and Allen poured a tablet

into it.

"Let me get you some water, pal." Allen reached toward the nightstand and came back holding a glass of water, bendy straw included. Niiice.

Zane popped the pill and chased it down with a pull from the straw. The water dusted grime from the back of his throat, leaving cool tracks in its wake. *Ahh.*

"Thanks."

"Anytime. It might make you a little dizzy so try not to get out of bed. Do you need some help to the bathroom before the medicine hits your bloodstream?"

Yeah, come to think of it he did. He swung his legs over the edge of the bed and decided to tell his pride to take a walk. Something told him he needed Allen's help, whether he liked it or not.

Leaning on the vet-doctor like the man was the only support in a gale force, he moved his feet in little-old-man shuffles to the bathroom. The damn things didn't move more than an inch at a time. By the time he finished his bathroom duties and shuffled his ass back to the bed, he swore an hour had passed. The Vicodin started to kick in, giving him a dose of lightheadedness and a slight bit of pain relief.

Allen patted Zane on the shoulder. "Try to get some rest. By the time the pill wears off and you wake up, you should feel better. Then I'll send in our alpha." His lips turned upward as a twinkle entered his eyes. "I think you'll get along just fine with her. See you later."

A click of the door and Zane was alone with a sliver of light, a glass of water and his thoughts. Which swam around in circles like hungry sharks. He kept following his prey, and every time he gave chase, the scent of his mate slapped through his senses, stopping him in his tracks.

Then he'd run after her, trying to catch a glimpse of her face, her body, anything besides her scent, but only found his prey watching him. The dream restarted, over and over again until he fell into a restless sleep.

****

Margie pressed her lips together in a painful attempt not to snap at Landa. The poor female walked like molasses traveling uphill on a cold day as she carried the tray of soup meant for the wounded alpha. She could have had an entire meeting with her elders and then watched Christmas whiz on past by the time Landa made it halfway down the infirmary hallway.

"I'm sorry, alpha. I don't want the soup to spill. He needs as much food as possible. It's not needed to walk beside me."

Sure and what was she supposed to do? Storm into the room containing the alpha, mention she brought him soup and then wait for freaking ever before it showed up?

Yes, yes, yes, her hormones clamored. *Damn hormones.* She could do without the things banging about in her body, making coming into heat seem like a walk in the park. Wait a minute, maybe she was going into heat, maybe the wounded alpha lying in the infirmary was just that, a wounded alpha and nothing more. *Yeah, right.* She might not like it, but that wolf belonged to her.

Shit.

"It's okay, Landa. I just need to see him." *Might as well see who fate threw me together with.* Her body tingled at the thought of her mate's hands stroking her skin, while her mind got busy passing out warning signals. *Run away, run away*. Geez, she didn't know what side to jump on, fear or hormonal irrationality.

Wasn't being a female grand?

A hint of a smile touched Landa's lips. "I understand."

Margie had a creepy feeling Landa understood way more than she should. Different werewolves possessed varying gifts ranging from none to telekinesis and everything in between. Perhaps Landa had a gift of reading minds.

Don't-ask-don't-tell needed a repeal.

She'd work on that, right after she saw the injured wolf.

Their footsteps echoed down the linoleum corridor located under the ranch house as the smell of cleaning solution filled her nose. Her father had been one smart male to build a virtual compound that doubled as a dude ranch. She closed her eyes as memories of her parents washed over her.

It had been ten years since they died in a car crash and for the most part she did well. Time healed wounds, even grievous ones. But occasionally a memory would sneak in, slip past the barriers erected, and reduce her to rubble. What made the scent of lemon-fresh cleaning solution and the clap of boot heels on linoleum that sneaky memory, she'd never know.

She would not allow the memory to bring grief and longing. *Nope. Not today*. Today she would meet her mate. A moment she wished she could share with her parents.

Damn. Enough with the parental memories. *Think mate, think mate.*

Allen thought the wounded were would be awake

now, the pain pill's effects worn off. Werewolf genetics sped the metabolism of pain medication, causing a dose that would tranquilize a human to burn through their bodies in a couple of hours. If luck held, the were, her alpha, her mate—that had a nice ring to it, mate— would be awake and able to tell her why he was here.

She seriously doubted Cupid sent him.

"How much farther, alpha?"

"Allen said the first door on the right once you're through the double doors." And as the double doors were right in front of them, Christmas had arrived. Margie grinned at her joke and slapped her palms against the bar, shoving the door open. Striding through first, she caught the door with the heel of her boot, holding it for Landa, who walked through hunched like a protective momma over the tray.

"We're here." Margie turned the handle and got her first glimpse of the wounded were in human form. Day-um, the male was hot. Even wounded and sporting a bandage wrapped around his muscular chest, he exuded a sensuality she felt herself drawn to. His hair was black, shot through with strands of silver and tan. Like a wolf pelt, not the silver of old age.

His eyes were closed, his nose long and aquiline, his cheekbones high and firm. A square jaw lined with thick stubble capped the rugged impression. His lower body lay under a sheet, leg bent at the knee, and she could see the outline of his rather impressive package.

Heat blossomed in her lower gut, warming her core, readying her for him. Oh right, like that was going to happen now. *Get a grip, Margie.* Damn overactive hormones, always popping up when they shouldn't.

"Hello? Zane?" Margie took a step into the room,

calling out his name. Zane. Allen told her his name when he updated her on his condition. Zane. According to fate, he belonged to her. Her skin heated and she closed her eyes. She did not need horny right now.

His eyes rolled open, amber depths staring at her in confusion. Maybe Allen was wrong, maybe it took this wolf longer to metabolize pain medication than it did her pack.

A soft brush of air heralded Landa's arrival into the room.

"Hey, I—"

Crash! Broken pieces of pottery shattered across the floor, soup splatters scattering to the corners of the room. Margie looked at the mess and then turned her gaze to Landa. Pale and trembling, Landa raised shaking hands to flutter over her mouth, her eyes wide as she stared at the male in the bed.

I'm so sorry, alpha, Landa said telepathically before turning and hauling ass back down the corridor.

What the hell? Margie choked on the scent of fear that lingered in the room. One glance at the bed showed formerly sleepy eyes opened and narrowed. He yanked the covers back and she got a glimpse of his package. Oh yeah, she had to get some of that.

Holy shit, Margie, enough of the hormones.

Shaking her head, trying to clear it of thoughts of hot, slick sex with the werewolf in front of her, she pointed her finger at the alpha.

"Don't move."

She darted out of the room, slamming the door behind her and pushed the external locking mechanism. A heavy body crashed against the door, the handle rattling, but she was running, shoving through the double doors like they didn't exist, following the sharp, acrid scent of fear down the corridor. Behind her she heard a howl, a shattering of the air. Good thing she had sense enough to lock Zane in his room until she figured out what was going on.

Running at full speed, she passed the tiny nursing enclave, the small indention in the wall. Empty now, it held a computer, a chair and a keypad with a big red button on the wall. Margie screeched to a halt, pivoting an about-face as she rushed back to the desk. Her father had the foresight to build these tunnels, but her mother had the foresight to lock them down. Margie slapped a hand over the button and heard the satisfying click of locks. Two breaths later, she heard another howl, this one from the direction of the stairs.

Margie stalked toward the stairs. Why run? Landa was going nowhere and neither was Zane. She mentally shredded the don't-ask-don't-tell policy the closer she got to Landa. The frantic pounding of fists against steel echoed down the stairs, joined by a suffocating stench of fear. Something petrified Landa and Margie had an awful suspicion it was Zane. Something about her new guest frightened her newest pack member and it sure as hell wasn't his rugged good looks.

Near the top, she saw Landa pounding on the door, her breath coming in small pants.

"Landa?"

The little blonde spun, eyes rolling white in their sockets, her hands held in front of her body. "Please, alpha, please don't make me go with him. Please, I beg of you. I'll do anything."

"Calm down and tell me what's going on."

"He's one of Sid's enforcers. I can't go back there,

I can't!" Her voice rose, high-pitched and frantic.

Sid? Margie tried to remember all the alphas in North America that she had either met or heard about and drew a big blank. Who the hell was Sid? "Is he the one that gave you the scar?"

Landa's left hand touched her throat. "Yes. He used magic to lock the band around my neck. Please don't make me go back."

As if that was an option.

"Do you seriously think that I would turn you over to him?"

Landa's lids did a slow open and shut. "You don't know Sid."

"You're right, I don't. But I do know that no pack member of mine is going to be torn away without a fight. What kind of a leader would I be if I just rolled over and let him take you?"

A flicker of surprise crossed Landa's face before she dropped to her knees. "Alpha, I meant you no disrespect. Sid's ... well, he's the most frightening thing I know."

Thing, eh? Guess that said a lot about the mysterious Sid. She really wanted to know who the hell this Sid guy was. Stop the presses, it was her lucky day. She had two people here who would tell her.

Laying a hand on Landa's shoulder, Margie squatted in front of the little blonde. "Why don't we go somewhere and talk?"

Bang! Metal rasped against metal, the noise warping through the hall and stairwell. Landa started shaking, one hand pressed against the scar at her throat. Margie rose to her feet. Apparently, the locked-down alpha was giving freedom an attempt. *Shit*.

Leaning around Landa, she punched the code in the keypad next to the door.

When the door unlocked, she helped Landa to her feet and gave her a little push through the doorway. "Landa, go find Allen and Big G and send them back here. Then go to my office and wait for me. Do you understand?"

Landa nodded. "I'll wait for you."

"Good. We are past due for a talk."

At the push of a button, the lock engaged, the pleasant sound of a bolt slamming home reverberating in her ears. Margie took in a deep breath and let it out. Being an alpha had its challenges, but this one presented the hardest challenge of her tenure.

The mate she'd never wanted terrorized her newest pack member simply by being the enforcer of a magic-crazed alpha she'd never met or heard of. Like they discussed this situation in the alpha handbook.

Crash! *Bang*! If she didn't stop him, he'd destroy her infirmary. Margie jogged down the stairs and ran toward Zane's room, stopping at the nursing station. Using the code and keypad, she unlocked the double doors leading to the infirmary wing and Zane, leaving the main door at the top of the stairs locked. To get into the wing, Allen would need to enter the code on the other side of the main door. *Wasn't security wonderful*?

Deep breath in, think calm thoughts. She pushed through the double doors, stopping in front of the alpha's room. It was now or never. She banged on the metal door.

"Hey, in there. I'm going to open the door. Don't even think about taking me down." As if he could. If she knew he was her mate, she assumed he could sense she was his. And mates would never hurt each other. Although if he wanted to take her down and sex her senseless she wouldn't oppose him.

Pull it together Margie! How can you think of sex at a time like this?

She shook her head—who would have thought meeting her mate would cause sexual thoughts to overwhelm her common sense—and rapped on the door. "Do you hear me?"

"I do. Why am I locked in?"

She liked his voice. Maybe she could get him to speak more just to hear the melodious rumble as it crossed her skin. By the saints, what was she thinking? *Hello, Margie, pull your head out of your hormones and channel your inner alpha.*

After she pushed the code into the keypad, she turned the knob and pushed open the door. Spilled soup lay in twisting rivulets across the floor, flowing from the broken bowl. Zane stood in front of the bed, arms crossed, completely naked with the exception of a silver torc around his neck. Oh yeah, she could get used to the eye candy. It was impressive.

Eye contact, Margie, eye contact.

Like meeting his eyes helped. Black brows and thick lashes framed amber eyes that gleamed with questions. Sleep-tussled hair hung in waves to his shoulders. Above a white bandage wrapped around his middle, tight curls dusted his chest and below the bandage the curls led in a trail from his navel to...

Eyes, Margie, eyes.

And while she was at it, she might as well wipe the blush off her face, which was easier thought than done.

"I'm Margie McLean, London's pack leader."

"Nice meeting you. I'm Zane Moskos, but you already know that, right?"

"Allen told me. Sorry about the lockdown. I had an issue I needed to deal with. Perhaps you'd be more comfortable sitting?" As if an alpha male, even one wounded, would take her up on the offer.

He remained standing, his gaze raking over her body. A tilt of his lips promised bliss from a male who knew what he wanted and how to get it. If Big G and Allen didn't hurry up, her hormones would have their way with Zane.

"How long has Landa been here?"

"How do you know her?"

Zane ran a hand through his hair, wincing as his arm rose. "I was sent to find and capture her."

Chapter Three

Margie's eyes narrowed and Zane felt the twisting tendrils of her anger wrap around him. Even pissed off she was the best thing he'd ever seen, although that must be mating hormones talking since nothing about her was his type. She stood around six feet tall with short brown hair cropped chin length and large eyes the color of good Scotch. He wanted to drink in her scent, to drag her beneath him and prove to her he was her alpha.

Oh, wait. He couldn't prove anything with Sid's damn torc on. The spell weaved into the twisted silver ensured the wearer's magic remained trapped, locked away, useless. Born an alpha, the torc reduced him to a beta. A beta with an alpha's scent and strength and none of his powers. The only way to get the thing off his neck was through death, his or Sid's.

And he sure as fuck wasn't dying anytime soon.

"Well now. If that's true, it seems you and I have a problem."

Yeah? Ya think? "Do we?"

"I'm not giving you Landa. She's part of my pack now. And I guard what's mine."

He'd like in on a little of that guarding action. "I said I was sent to find and capture her, not that I wanted to."

"Great! Then just say no and leave her here in

peace."

He'd like nothing more than to do just that, but Sid held his sister as collateral, thereby ensuring he'd return. Prey in hand. The bastard.

"As much as I'd love to do that, I can't."

"Can't or won't?"

"Can't."

"Well, then. We're back to our problem."

He shrugged and stared at her, liking the way her hair brushed her jaw, noting the muscles twitching in her legs under her jeans. Maybe she was thinking of giving him a kick in the ass with those steel-toed shit-kickers she wore.

He didn't really blame her.

He wanted to kick himself in the ass.

"Is it true what they say about you?"

One eyebrow cocked a droll tune. "What? That I'm a hard-nosed bitch?"

"Nope. That you know a bit of magic."

Well, didn't that deflate the wind out of her sails. If her face got any paler, she'd pass for a ghost. Her eyes widened as they met his gaze. A flash of fear sparked and dissipated. "What makes you think I'd know anything about magic?"

Not a thing like Sid. Sid enjoyed lording his magical abilities over others. Margie seemed to hide from hers. Provided she had any. Maybe the rumors he heard were wrong.

"When I got close to London, Montana, a few people started describing how you knew some magic. The magic alpha bitch, I believe it was said."

"Who—" Her voice squeaked and she cleared it. "Who said that?"

Zane shrugged. "Some drunk were at a bar in Billings."

"Oh, that's just great." One hand ran through her hair, ruffling it. She started pacing in front of him, over to the soup mess, back to the clean floor, again to the soup. The same hand ran another stroke through her hair. "Why does Sid want Landa so badly?"

Zane heard his teeth click together, his jaw clenched so hard. He pictured his sister, Zenia, as he'd last seen her, the band Landa had worn clamped around her neck, her eyes full of pain and fear. "He's a sick son of a bitch. He sees a female he wants and he takes her. Keeps her caged like a dog, collar and all. Somehow Landa escaped. Sid wants her back."

"What kind of sick person are you to take a female back to those types of conditions?" Her eyes narrowed, the glare she gave him piercing like a spear.

"Unless you have magical abilities and want to help me take this thing off, I don't have a choice." Sticking a finger through his torc, he pulled, the metal biting into his neck. "This damn thing ensures I stay nothing more than a lackey. Until I get rid of it, I have no choice. If I don't come back with Landa, Sid will torture my sister, my twin. What would you do?"

Margie's brows shot upward, but before she could answer, the metallic click of security doors opening followed by heavy footsteps echoed down the hall.

"Well, well, what do we have here? How you doing, Zane?" Allen strode into the room like he owned the place—which he probably did seeing they stood in the infirmary.

Zane took a deep breath, trying to shove the anger down. He needed Margie to take the fucking torc off his neck so he could man-up and grow the alpha pair he'd been born with. And he was doing a piss-poor job of convincing her.

He glared at Allen, until he got a look-see at what came in the door behind the vet-doctor. The mountain of a were had a shaved head, tats on his neck, arms, and knuckles, and who the hell knew where else, and a don't-fuck-with-me expression on his face.

Like that was an option.

Impressive.

So this was who carried him from the woods to his current residence. A skinhead giant on steroids. Without a doubt one of Margie's enforcers.

"Fine." The word spat off his tongue.

"Zane needs his bandage checked and he needs to stay down here until I can figure out what to do about this whole thing." Margie gestured around the room.

The giant cracked a shit-eating smile and popped his knuckles. "I'll be happy to take care of him."

"Just make sure he stays in the room, Big G. Don't touch him unless he tries to leave."

The grin disappeared on a sigh. "As you wish, alpha."

"Hey—"

"Don't worry, Zane. I'll be back for you. And somebody find the cleaning staff to clean up this mess." She pointed to the spilled soup and marched out the door.

If his jaw got any more tense, it would snap in half.

Allen slapped a palm against his shoulder. "Don't worry, pal. She'll be back. On second thought, maybe you should worry about that. She looked like she just stepped in a cow patty."

And the shit's name was Zane.

What a way to meet his mate.

****

Could this day get any worse? Had her mate truly aligned himself with an alpha who aspired to be the were equivalent of Hitler? If she helped Zane, what would happen to her and her pack? Who else had this problem that she could turn to for advice? Someone, anyone? Like the answer was suddenly going to pop into her head. *Nope*. She was on her own.

Situations like this made her hate being an alpha.

No time for a pity party. If she wanted to make a decision, she needed all the facts. And part of those facts sat upstairs in her office.

Margie hit the stairs leading out of the underground infirmary two at a time and slammed her hands against the release bar of the door. Which did absolutely nothing. Looked like Allen had locked the door behind him.

Yet another reason to like that vet-doctor.

After a punch of the code, she bolted through the door into the staff hallway of the main ranch house. Three doors down and there was her office, Landa parked in one of the leather chairs in front of the desk. Her head turned as Margie slammed the door shut and strode across the room.

With any luck Landa's speech would sway her one way or another. Because as it stood now, she wavered between helping Zane rid himself of the torc—assuming he told the truth about that piece of neckwear—and telling him what he could do with the thing.

Have a mate or save her pack from danger.

What a choice.

Taking a seat in her leather swivel chair, she propped her boots on the desk and crossed her arms. "Talk."

Landa gulped and clasped her hands so tight, Margie heard the knuckles crack. Pity for the wolf warred with the knowledge her pack might be in danger due to whatever happened in Landa's past.

If only she'd rescinded the don't-ask-don't-tell policy. Coulda, woulda, shoulda got one all of nowhere fast.

"What would you like to know?" Good thing Margie had excellent hearing. Landa's whispered words barely made it across the span of the desk.

"Start at the beginning. And Landa," the blonde wolf's gaze flicked to hers, "you are not going with Zane. Do you understand? You. Are not. Going. With him."

Tears formed in Landa's eyes and she dashed them away as her gaze dropped to her lap. A deep breath in. And the words tumbled out.

"My pack was overtaken by Sid's some time ago. When I reached maturity, he saw me and liked what he saw." She swallowed and touched her neck. "He kept me on a leash attached to a collar. He cast a spell on it so I couldn't just take it off and leave."

Margie felt a snarl turn her lip and she had to take a deep breath to calm herself enough to speak. "Then how did you escape?"

The corners of Landa's lips turned up. "He thought I was stupid so he left his grimoire lying out. When he'd leave the room, I'd study his magic." Her gaze flicked to Margie's and held steady. "I learned the counter-spell to release the collar and ran. Kept running until I got here."

"Your family?"

Landa shuddered, her gaze dropping to her clasped hands. "They're dead," she whispered. "He killed them all."

Margie's feet hit the floor with a thud and she leaned forward, resting her forearms on the desk. "I'm sorry."

Landa nodded. Her eyes squeezed shut as air whistled into her lungs. "Thank you. Sid can't stand to lose. It's a pride thing. I thought I covered my tracks, but I didn't have a chance against Zane. I'm so sorry," her gaze met Margie's. "I've brought trouble upon your pack."

"Our pack. So tell me about Zane." The thought that her mate was somehow aligned with a cruel leader didn't sit well in her gut. Although he had said his sister was being held by Sid. And due to an apparently magical-powered torc, he didn't have a choice in the matter.

What kind of alpha didn't have a choice in the matter?

And what the hell did that torc have to do with it?

"Zane is one of Sid's enforcers. I don't know him well."

"Why does he wear that torc?"

"Sid weaves magic into those torcs and then he puts them on all the alpha males born in the pack when they reach puberty. It keeps their alpha powers locked."

Oh, hell no. She did not just hear that. Her view of Sid hit dirt bottom and kept right on barreling downward.

Her growl was interrupted by footsteps beating a fast rhythm down the hall, pausing outside her office door.

Bang! Bang! Bang! "Alpha!"

Jace didn't bother with such niceties as waiting for her to give the okay to open the door. Nope. He burst in like his boots were on fire and the only extinguisher was in her office.

"What's wrong?"

"There was someone in the woods, where we found that injured wolf last night. He roughed Mike up and said that he was here for the others. We're takin' Mike to the infirmary now."

"What? How roughed up? And what the hell was Mike doing in the woods?"

Mike wasn't even an enforcer. As a pack member who lived on the dude ranch, his responsibilities involved helping take care of the horses.

"One of the mares took off so he chased her to the fence line. Said that some guy was on the other side of the fence and when he asked him what he was doing, the dude shot something at him. Didn't physically touch him, but Mike looks like a vampire left out in the sun. It's bad."

"Sid," Landa whispered, eyes gone wide.

"What did he do to Mike?" Margie turned to Landa.

"Sounds like he threw an energy ball. It's one of his specialties."

Not for long it wasn't. Sid had gone from being someone else's dictator to moving his game into her territory.

And nobody messed with her pack.

So hell yeah, she was going to cast a counter-spell to whatever magic Sid had working in Zane's torc. He'd brought the fight here, and everything in her cried out to take him down.

He was about to discover how dangerous it was to cross a female alpha.

Chapter Four

Zane paced from one end of his room to the other, his bare feet slapping against the cool tile of linoleum, borrowed scrub bottoms tied around his hips. The janitor had come and gone and the spot on the floor previously covered in soup now gleamed like ice on a sunny day. Allen had left in a hurry what felt like a lifetime ago and Big G stood in the hall, the door wide open.

Not like he could leave. He might not have the white bandage wrapped around his chest, but he still had stitches and an unhealed hole where the bullet went in.

And he wanted to see Margie again.

Even if she was still mad at him.

As if the higher powers heard him and decided to be accommodating for once, Margie put in an appearance, her boots tapping an angry rhythm on the linoleum. She slapped a palm on Big G's shoulder as she walked into the room.

"Thanks for watching."

"Anytime, alpha."

She flicked her wrist and the door closed, shutting them in together. Alone. With his mate. Who looked madder than a bull about to be castrated.

So the higher powers were only partially accommodating.

"I just saw one of my pack members lying in a bed, badly burned due to an energy blast apparently thrown by Sid."

"Sid's here?" What? Did the fucker not trust him to bring Landa back? This just proved that Sid was smarter than he seemed.

"You know anyone else that can throw an energy blast? 'Cuz I sure don't."

"Can you?"

"Throw energy around?"

He nodded once.

Margie's lips turned up like she knew a secret and she shrugged. "Tell me about the torc. Landa touched on it, but I want to know exactly what it does."

Zane stuck his finger under the torc and yanked. Nothing happened except the bite of metal against his neck. "It won't come off. Sid weaved magic into the metal which..." he paused, not wanting to admit he was weaker than he should be, that his powers were tied and try as he might he could do nothing about it. "Um, it means that he has power over me. Also means he can find whoever's wearing the damn thing."

"What kind of power over you?"

Yeah, right, like he wanted to go into that one. Admitting he had no powers was a slap to his pride.

"Look, Zane. If you want me to break the spell, you need to tell me exactly what it does. Skirting around the problem doesn't work with magic."

Zane ran a hand through his hair and tilted his head back so he stared at the ceiling. No help from that quarter. If getting free of the torc meant a slap to his pride, it was worth it.

Despite the fact it made him look weak in front of

his mate.

"It binds my alpha powers. When an alpha reaches puberty, Sid puts one of these torcs around their necks. We have the strength and scent of an alpha, but none of the powers that go along with it. For all basic purposes we live our lives as betas and become his enforcers."

Margie snarled. *Snarled*. And damn him, but it was hot as hell to know she was upset over his neckwear.

"Okay, this guy is going down. Why hasn't any other pack wised up to what he's been doing?"

"He's good at hiding his tracks. And we live in an isolated part of South Dakota, so there's not a lot of interaction with other packs."

"How long has this been going on?"

"He took over the pack around the time my parents first mated. They said at first it wasn't so bad, but then he got mixed up with magic and went into dictator mode and after that happened, things went downhill fast. Are you going to help me get rid of this thing?" He did another round of the finger-pulling-the-torc routine.

"He put one of my pack members in the infirmary and we might have to move him to a human hospital. So if you want me to help you kick his ass all the way to the ocean, I'm happy to oblige."

Nice to know the earlier blow to his pride turned out so well.

"It's appreciated."

Margie nodded, the anger in her eyes bleeding to determination. "Landa mentioned a grimoire. Besides tossing energy blasts and binding alpha powers, what other tricks does he have up his sleeves?"

She was actually going to help him. The tightness in his chest relaxed. Sure, the stitches binding the bullet hole together were still there, but the powerlessness he felt over not being able to save his twin eased. Help from one's mate tended to do that to a wolf.

"I don't know. He keeps females locked up like dogs. Like he did Landa. Like he is Zenia." Zane dragged in a breath. "But that magic seems to be similar to the torcs'. He has no problems killing those who get in his way. Usually by blasting them with energy."

"So, we have an energy blasting dictator who maintains his reign of terror by non-discretionary killing."

"That pretty much sums it up."

"Well, a bullet can kill anything. Provided it has a chance."

"Fairly certain that's been tried before. It didn't work."

"We'll see. Now let me look at that torc."

****

Margie walked up to Zane, drinking in the anticipation glowing in his amber eyes. This close she could see the shadow of a beard on his cheeks, smell the scent of evergreens that belonged to him alone. Her skin simmered from the heat of his body, dancing shivers of warmth tracing the veins in her limbs. Her body spoke to his in the most ancient of ways, the calling of alpha-to-alpha, mate-to-mate. She wanted to stretch out on the bed and explore every inch of him.

She needed to find a way to take the torc off his neck.

Damn responsibilities.

Reaching out, she tucked her forefinger under the torc and ran her thumb across the twisted metal, a tremor shooting through her body at the touch. The heat of his skin warmed the back of her hand and instead of focusing on the metal, she turned her attention to his eyes. Amber irises watched her from under lowered lids.

"What do you think?" His breath caressed her cheek and she felt liquid pool between her legs.

That the bed's three feet away and the door is shut. "I feel the magical signature, but will need some time to figure out the spell he placed on it."

"How long? If Sid's here, he won't hesitate to attack you."

"I know. I'm not sure how long it will take. Sit over there." She took a step back and gestured to the bed.

A smile creaked across his lips. "While I'd love to see you in my bed, I'm not sure now is the time."

"Oh, I—," Margie took a deep breath and tried to will away the blush attempting to turn her face a nice shade of tomato. No such luck. "Just sit. So I can look at the torc."

His smile broadened. "Just for you." Zane walked to the bed and sat, his gaze never leaving hers.

Ah. Now she liked that picture, hot, shirtless, alpha male on a bed. *Good one, Margie. Your pack is under attack and all you can think about is sex. What the hell is wrong with you?*

Throughout her life she'd heard about finding one's mate and the hormonal shift that occurred, but until she saw Zane, she hadn't realized how strong the biological urge was. Until last night, she hadn't even wanted a mate.

But now, within hours of meeting him, she couldn't imagine life without him. She wanted him in her bed, in her life, in her body. Especially in her body.

Talk about an abrupt shift in thought patterns. Teenagers and menopausal women had nothing on her.

Zane inhaled deeply, his jaw tensing, a blast of heat flowing from him. Great. He must have smelled her arousal. She ventured a gaze down his body. Yep. Definitely smelled her arousal and was reacting accordingly.

Magic, Margie, focus on the magical signature and how to counteract it.

Two steps and she stood in front of him, her fingers locking around the torc. Closing her eyes, she pictured the magical signature that twisted through the metal. Threads of red mixed with strands of silver, woven into the metal like braiding on a sweater. Amazing. And daunting.

For while she had learned magic, she had never seen anything like this. Energy balls, fog, making people do things they wouldn't normally do, no problem. Imbuing inanimate objects with magical abilities, big problem. Sure, she'd heard of it. But it was a magic she hadn't bothered to study. What was the point?

As her mother wisely said, just because you can doesn't always mean you should.

So now she needed to learn how to break the spell on Zane's torc when she had no previous experience using that type of magic. No one did. No one—

Her eyes popped open. She might not know how to get the damn torc off Zane's neck, but Landa might. The little wolf had read Sid's grimoire and freed herself. Landa knew magic too.

"Zane?"

"Mmm?" Lust-riddled eyes met her gaze and heat slammed into her.

"If this torc comes off, what happens to Landa?"

"If you get this torc off, she won't have to worry about Sid because he'll be dead. By my hand."

"And if it doesn't come off?"

"If you can't block the magic, then you'll need to keep me away from the fight. Sid will try to control me if he sees me."

"Do we need to tie you up?"

"Mmm." He waggled his brows. "Only if you want to, babe."

Margie shook her head and sighed with a loud huff. Tease. Her thoughts went careening down a path that had nothing to do with Sid's impending attack and everything to do with seeing Zane tied to a bed, his body eager for hers. *Head back in the game, Margie.* "When's the best time to attack? Provided he's still outside my property."

"Oh, he's still there. He has Landa in his sights and he won't let her go. Assume he didn't come alone either. He'd have left half his enforcers at home and half of them he'll have with him."

"How many?"

"Twelve total. So that means he'll have six here. Expect a fight."

"Do the enforcers stay with him because they want to or because they have to?"

"Most don't want to, but some are like Sid. They'll follow him willingly."

"Maybe we can help the rest of them. If Sid wasn't already here, I'd call in different alphas to help out. They'd love a fight with a dictator."

"Come here." One minute she was in the middle of a discussion and the next, his hand clasped around her wrist, drawing her to him. His arms encircled her waist as he flipped her onto her back on the bed, his heavy body following, his lips pressing against hers.

Oh, yeah. She wanted this, wanted him. Her arms wrapped around his back, pressing him closer, while her lips opened for the thrust of his tongue. The kiss was anything but gentle, a claiming of alpha-to-alpha, male-to-female. Each stroke plundered her mouth, her soul, marking her as his.

One hand ran between her breasts and down her side, searching and finding the hem of her shirt. With a quick flick of his wrist, her shirt moved out of the way and his hand traced across the skin of her stomach. When he pushed aside the cup of her bra and rolled her nipple between his fingers, she let loose a moan.

Hers. She belonged to him and he to her. *Forever.*

Once she accepted him as her mate, once she allowed him in her body, they became each other's, for in the pack there was no divorce, no separation. Once a were found his or her mate, they stayed together until they died. If things continued on the path they were heading, the two would soon be mated.

No matter that Sid was running around the vicinity of her pack, or that she really needed to be working on getting that torc off Zane's neck. Mating hormones prevailed. She wanted him, he obviously wanted her and that was that.

Or not. Instead of mating with Zane now, she had pack responsibilities. She needed to ensure Sid didn't kill a single one of her pack members. She needed to be in on the fight. Mating could come later.

Margie pushed at Zane's shoulders until he raised his head and looked at her with a puzzled gaze.

"Sid's out there now threatening my pack. I should be preparing for a fight, not mating."

Zane pressed his forehead against hers as he drew in several deep breaths while smoothing her bra cup over her breast. Despite its covering, the skin of her breast felt cold from the lack of his touch. "You're right," came out as a growl, "but I don't want you to leave."

"Come with me to talk to the pack. Provided Allen released you?"

Zane raised his head and looked her dead on. "I release myself. He removed the bandage. I have stitches and I heal fast. And Sid's my kill."

Margie pecked him on the lips as he started to stand.

"Keep that up my little wolf and you won't be leaving this room anytime soon."

"Mmm. I'll have to remember that." She took his hand and he pulled her to her feet. "Let's get you a shirt and shoes and then we'll meet with my pack. They should know what's going on."

****

Zane watched Margie as she strode to a wardrobe and pulled out a scrub top. Her ass was made for his hands to grasp as she rode him, while her slick core gripped his staff. He shook his head, dispelling the fantasy. As much as he hated to admit it, Margie was right. They did not need to be mating while Sid was terrorizing her pack.

Intellectually he knew that, but the mating hormones rode through his veins like a wave of lust and

124

his higher thought ground to almost a complete halt. Once they neutralized the threat of Sid, he would finish what they started, claiming her as his. But by then he would be free of the torc and could claim her as an alpha, not as the beta enforcer he was now.

Margie pitched him the scrub top and Zane pulled it over his head. Who would have thought he'd rock the doctor look?

"Hey, check me out. I'm the good doctor Ben Dover, proctologist."

Margie barked a short burst of laughter. "Oh my gosh, I can't believe you just said that."

"I can't believe I'm wearing this get-up."

"It's easy to get to since it's right here in the room. You need shoes, though. Hmm. Here are some socks. We have the standard slippers, but I'm going to have to ask someone to loan you a pair of shoes."

He liked watching her think. Or move. Or, well, he liked everything about her so far. And now that he had a taste of her, he wanted more. There would be plenty of time to taste her, to join with her, to be gloved by her core and her soul. Plenty of time once he got the damn torc removed and his alpha powers restored.

Provided the torc hadn't permanently suppressed his powers. Zane shuddered. Nope. Not going there. *Positive thoughts, Zane.*

After handing him a pair of baby blue hospital slippers, Margie moved to the door. He looked like a candidate for a geriatric commercial in his beige socks and baby blue slippers. On the plus side, the slippers barely made a sound as he walked by Margie's side.

Her boots and the soles of Big G's shit-kickers tapped an angry tune as they marched down the hall.

"You sure he should be out walking around, alpha?"

"Yes, Big G, I'm sure. When we get to the top of the stairs, I'll need you to call the pack together. I need everyone to meet inside, on the basketball court. Outside is dangerous with Sid around. Zane, we have a couple that resides off this property. Would Sid try to take them out, or is he more likely to focus here?"

"He wouldn't expect pack members to live anyplace other than in the direct vicinity of the alpha. They should be safe where they are."

Margie slammed her palms against the release bar on the door at the top of the stairs and strode through, turning to Big G.

"Big G. Don't call in Tom and Vonda. They should be safer where they're at, but do let them know to be on the lookout for Sid."

"How do you know he is telling the truth?" Big G nodded in Zane's direction. Zane couldn't blame the giant for doubting him, nor could he stop the snarl from crossing his lips for the insult.

"He's my mate."

"Well, hell. That means I have to play nice, don't it?"

Margie patted him on the shoulder. "Go on now. Make sure everyone on the ranch is gathered in thirty minutes. I'll be in my office with Zane and Landa."

She marched in the opposite direction from the giant. Zane narrowed his gaze on Big G and started to turn when the giant hissed at him.

"You might be her mate, which one day will make you my alpha, but alpha or no, you fuck with her and I'll rip your throat out." His canines flashed as he snarled at Zane before striding off down the hall.

Zane growled, wanting to run after Big G, wanting to avenge the disrespect. His feet apparently liked that plan too as his baby blues turned in Big G's direction. But that route meant he was nothing better than Sid. Avenging disrespect, fighting for honor, destroying other lives. All because his ego pride couldn't handle a bit of truth.

What was he? A spoiled child or a full-grown male?

And shouldn't he be glad to know Margie's enforcers were willing to go up against her mate if he hurt her? Most definitely.

Stinging pride was a dangerous thing.

Instead of talking to Big G about the giant's attitude, he should be getting busy earning that respect. Earning it. Not demanding it. Demanding it would only cause dissension and dissension within the pack damaged pack dynamics.

After all, Big G's job was to protect his alpha, Margie. True loyalty by an enforcer was hard to come by, he should know. If Margie managed through trust and respect to inspire loyalty in her followers, then what right did he have to interfere? Even if it meant sucking down insults and disrespect.

Oh shit. He was going to have his own pack. *This one*. Complete with the skinhead giant enforcer his pride wanted a piece of. Why hadn't he thought of that sooner? How would he run a pack? The only example he had was the dictator from hell. Okay, so he knew enough not to go that route. Other than that, he had abso-fucking-lutely no idea how to do it. Luckily for him, his mate seemed to know what to do. The few wolves he'd met today had shown Margie only loyalty and respect.

Learning from her was his number two priority, right after removing the damn torc from around his neck. No, wait. Learning from her was number three on his to-do list, number two being a horizontal work-out session on the bed of her choice.

Oh, yeah. That was some action he wanted to get in on.

Now.

Unfortunately, he had the little matter of his neckwear amputation to attend to first.

His slippers swished on the wood floor as he turned and followed Margie into an office, his thoughts bouncing from one thing to the next. The ping-pong internal conversation came to an abrupt halt as he saw Landa sitting in an overstuffed leather chair, her upper body twisted around so she faced him, her face a ghostly white. Her eyes darted to Margie.

"You said I didn't have to go with him."

"And I mean that. This is your pack now. But he's not going back to Sid. He's my mate and I'm not going to let anyone else have power over him. So we're going to take his torc off. And you're going to help me."

Chapter Five

Margie watched Landa's eyes grow large, saw her throat move as she swallowed. "Me?" Her voice came out on a high-pitched squeak.

Margie toed the door shut and left Zane standing by it as she walked toward the blonde wolf. "I need your help, Landa. You read Sid's grimoire. You know more about him and his magic than I do. I know magic, but I don't know how to remove Zane's torc. I need you to show me. Are you willing to help me?"

Landa's gaze darted to Zane—who wisely stood still next to the closed door—her tongue licking her lips before her eyes closed. She pulled in a deep breath and opened her eyes, her gaze on Margie as she spoke.

"Are you sure he's your mate?"

Well, she hadn't expected that question. A simple yes or no-way-in-hell, sure. What did Zane being her mate have to do with it?

"I'm positive. Why?"

"Fate has a way of things, eh?"

"Will you help me or not, Landa?"

"What will he do when the torc is removed?"

"Kill the bastard." The growled words came from the door and Margie glanced to Zane. His lips pulled back in a snarl, his canines gleaming. "He took from me too, Landa, and for that I apologize. Because of this torc I was unable to save you when he took you for his.

Several of us tried to free you, but he stopped us before we were able. The punishment didn't mean we gave up trying. We never gave up trying. He deserves to pay for what he has done. Please. Help me to help you."

Muted tweets of birds drifted through the closed window into the vacuum of silence previously known as her office. Not that she blamed Landa for thinking on the matter. Zane had come for the little wolf, after all. If he hadn't been her mate, she might not have trusted him either. But even though they hadn't joined bodies, she felt as if she knew his mind, and she knew he wouldn't betray them no matter what happened.

Landa continued to stare at Zane as the minutes ticked by. Patience might be a virtue, but whoever wrote that proverb probably wasn't sitting around with his heart in his throat waiting for an answer.

Right when Margie opened her mouth to try again with the question, Landa's gaze turned to her.

"He speaks the truth. I'll help you."

Margie released a breath of air. Apparently patience really was a virtue. Not to mention it seemed like Landa really did read minds, which was something that bore watching in the future. "Great. Thank you. I have no clue about the torc. I can feel its magic and that's about it. Did you read the spell in Sid's grimoire?"

Landa nodded, her eyes focused on the white knuckles of her hands, her lips moving silently.

Margie waited for a minute. Nothing, but muted birdcalls. To hell with the proverb. "And?"

Landa's gaze flashed to hers and Margie hissed a breath in. Did her eyes turn black when she worked magic? Who knew? It wasn't like she looked in a mirror while casting spells. Landa's once blue irises now shone black as obsidian. Part of Margie expected Landa's head to start spinning around and her voice to warp.

She was only mildly disappointed when Landa's head stayed in place as she nodded at Margie. Rising from where she sat, Landa walked over to Zane, Margie trailing behind like a hungry dog on the scent of a rabbit. She saw magic twisting around Landa in ribbons of color, saw it circle around a wide-eyed pale-faced Zane. Damn, but the little wolf could work some magic. How long had she studied Sid's grimoire? Margie had worked hard learning magic spells, all under her parents' noses. She learned her magic through many hours of practice, but she had a feeling Landa's magic was part of her, strengthened by study.

'Cuz sure as she wore boots, ribbons of magic never visited her. Not once. If Landa learned this from Sid's grimoire, how the hell was Margie going to defeat him?

She stared at the colored ribbons surrounding Landa as the blonde touched the torc. Zane stiffened, his jaw tensing as if he was in pain. Ribbons of magic coalesced in Landa's palm, running into the torc as she touched it with her fingers. The magic hummed as it spread across the torc, vibrating colors surrounding Zane's neck. Tendons stood out in his arms as his fists clenched, his nostrils flaring.

The burning scent of pain filled the air, slamming into her like a punch to the ribs. Margie moved, a growl escaping her lips. She wanted to attack the one who hurt her mate, wanted to hurt Landa like she hurt Zane. But if she shredded Landa's flesh, Zane might be injured accidentally. Who knew what would happen if the spell broke while the spell-caster was in the middle of it.

How the hell did mated werewolves stop themselves from going insane every time anything happened to their mate? Instead of walking forward to rip Landa to shreds, she forced a step backward, then another and another until her leg hit one of the chairs. Margie grabbed the back of the chair, her hand turning into a claw as she punctured the leather.

Shredding leather chairs kept her from shredding her newest pack member.

As Landa waved her hands around Zane's head and neck, the magic rose in pitch, the humming vibrating at such a high frequency that Margie turned her claw back into a hand and clasped both palms over her ears. Zane howled, a scream of pain that echoed through the room. The sound beat through Margie's bones as the frequency of the magic changed. Higher and higher it rose until it shattered in an ear-splitting, headache-inducing bang, the torc dropping to the floor with a thud.

Landa sucked in a breath as the ribbons of magic dissipated into the air. Zane slumped against the wall and Margie raced to his side, kicking the torc out of the way.

"Zane! Are you okay?" Margie grabbed his arm and shook it, watching as his chest rose and fell. At least he lived.

"Is he ... well?" Landa gasped, crawling to where Zane lay.

"He's breathing. What did you do? I've never seen a spell like that."

"It was different than the band I wore. The magic was more ingrained with his essence. I'm not sure how he'll be when he wakes."

"How he'll be?"

"Sid trapped their powers, his enforcers. They all should have been alphas, but the torcs suppressed and contained their powers. When I removed the torc, the barrier to Zane's powers was removed, but I'm not sure if that means his alpha powers were also removed, or if they are ... coming online so to speak."

Zane moaned and Margie rubbed his arm. "Zane?"

His eyelids fluttered, opening with all the speed of a turtle. "What—"

"Landa removed the torc." Margie stroked the hair off his forehead. "How do you feel?"

His forehead knotted into a collage of lines. "Like all my blood was drained and replaced with fire." He struggled to sit upright, waving off Margie's hand. "But it's starting to feel better."

"The torc is gone, but I'm not sure what happened to your alpha powers." Landa fisted her hands in her lap. "You're free of Sid, but I just don't know about the rest of it."

Zane's fingers grasped Margie's, his thumb running over her knuckles. He gave her a wink, a half smile on his lips. "Thank you for getting it off, Landa. Whatever happens, at least I'm free of Sid."

"Do you feel like coming to the pack meeting?" Margie patted the back of his hand.

One eyebrow tried to meet his hairline. "Of course."

Males. Shoot them with bullets, zap them with magic ribbons and they keep right on going, pretending there were no problems. No matter what you did to them, their response remained, "it's merely a flesh wound, no big deal." It might be annoying if she didn't have so much respect for him.

She'd probably still be ass down on the ground instead of getting to her feet like Zane.

He put a muscular arm around her shoulders, drawing her against him. Small tremors ran from his arm into her shoulders as he reached a hand to help Landa up.

Ah, so he wasn't as impervious as he seemed.

Margie opened the door, glancing over her shoulder at Landa, catching the blonde with her hands behind her back. Landa's eyes popped wide seconds before she dropped her gaze and brought her hands to her front, straightening her shirt. If not for the flash of guilt crossing her face, there wouldn't have been anything unusual in the gesture.

Don't-ask-don't-tell might be repealed, but she couldn't hold up the pack meeting to discover what Landa had going on. For all Margie knew, she caught the blonde scratching her bum.

"I'll close the door, alpha."

Right, she might want to get a move on instead of standing in the hall staring into her office.

"Thanks, Landa."

Margie held onto Zane's waist as they walked down the hall, Landa walking a respectful distance behind them. The farther they walked, the stronger Zane became, until his arm no longer shook and he didn't need to lean on her.

But he still kept an arm around her shoulders.

She liked the heavy feel of his arm, liked the heat

as it radiated into her body. Maybe it was the hormones, or maybe it was the male, but she wanted this mating.

Obviously the hormones talking, as she didn't want to give up the running of her pack. This was her pack. Not his. Selfish? Most definitely. But then, she'd done a good job running it, if she said so herself.

When her father died, and she fought for alpha status, she had to prove herself, like every new pack leader. Just because she had been the previous alpha's daughter, didn't mean she had a free ride to the leader's chair. Nope. She'd worked hard to inspire trust and gain respect.

It might be selfish, but she didn't want to share.

She wanted her pack and her mate. Was that too much to ask? Apparently so. Guess it was time to learn how to share.

"Where's this basketball court?" Zane's eyes twinkled at her.

Why did he have to go all smiling and twinkling-eyed? Her insides melted with one glance from him. With any luck Sid would be gone soon, meaning she and Zane could finish what they'd started in the infirmary.

Margie let the smile break over her face. "It's in the gym. We're in the main ranch house now. The gym's a couple hundred yards in the back."

Dropping her arm from around Zane's waist, she pushed open the door leading to the outside. Zane caught it, holding it open for Landa, his arm falling back to his side. Residual heat slipped away from her shoulders, leaving her chilled in the evening air.

In one day she'd gone from never wanting a mate, to being unable to imagine life without one. Wouldn't the elders be pleased? She'd find the answer to that question in just a moment.

The sound of her pack's voices reached her ears before she touched the door to the gym. Zane held the door open for her to walk through and she marched into the chaos of voices, he and Landa trailing behind.

Her pack of forty sat on bleachers, their nervous voices rising and falling like the hum of insects on a hot summer day. Some knew what was happening, others only knew about Mike's injuries, and all were worried. She rarely called meetings like this. The last one had been when the pack tried to take Elizabeth, Tom's daughter, to live with them.

The biggest mistake of her leadership. Embarrassment still stained her cheeks at the thought. What she had been thinking was clear. How those thoughts translated into actions were another matter. Her reasons remained. All werewolves should band together, live together, not apart.

That's why she sent Big G and Jace to have Elizabeth returned to the pack. Elizabeth would turn furry while Tom never had. It had been her mistake to assume Tom knew why Big G and Jace had come for the girl. How was she supposed to know that Tom's mother never explained his recessed werewolf genetics? Margie rarely saw Tom and the grocery store aisle was not the place for a conversation on their heritage.

Luckily for her everything turned out well. Apologizes were made and accepted. Tom mated Vonda and the mating caused his werewolf genetics to come front and center. The two were now cherished members of the pack. Although Margie was glad to note they weren't here. Unlike the rest of her pack, they lived on Tom's ranch.

Tonight she would lead her pack to the edge of danger and hopefully things would go as well as the last time she called a meeting.

Someone saw her and started a wave of silence that rolled through the gym like a blackout. The click of Landa's boots as she walked across the wooden floor to park it on the front row echoed in the enclosed space. Who imagined she'd ever draw comfort from a mate standing by her side?

Margie sucked down a deep breath, facing her pack. God help them all, they were going to need all the celestial aid they could get.

"Thank you for coming." As if they had a choice. Alpha spoke and the pack jumped to follow. But still, it paid to be polite. "I have bad news. Perhaps you've heard about Mike?" Judging by the murmurs, a good deal of people, if not the whole pack, knew. "Mike was injured by a demented pack leader named Sid. Sid kept Landa chained and she barely escaped him." Landa's face flamed as the pack turned her way, shock scattered across their faces.

"Zane, the were we rescued last night, was sent after her, but refuses to return to Sid. Now Sid is here and wants what he thinks is his. We need to stop him. We need to ensure that what he did to Landa never happens to another female. Does anyone have objections to us taking him down?"

Murmurs abounded, but no objections. At least not to Sid.

"How do you know Zane isn't lying? That this isn't a trap?"

She expected that question, expected it and knew

the answer. Things would change once she opened her mouth. The sharing she feared would start. She was alpha. She was brave. Really. Sharing was a good thing. "Zane's my mate. I know he's not lying because I sense no deceit through the mating bond."

A pack of hunters could have run through the gym and no one would have moved after that little news ditty. The entire pack, from the children to the elders, stared at her like she'd returned from the dead. Then as one their faces morphed into grins as cheers broke out.

Embarrassing. Obviously the elders weren't the only ones who thought she needed to get a move on the mate hunt. At least they had a bit of happy news before Sid came to break up the party.

"Okay, okay. We'll talk about that one later. But suffice it to say, I know Zane's not double crossing us. Sid's out there. And we're going to stop him."

****

Zane watched his mate discuss ways to stop Sid, watched her interaction with her pack. *His pack*. He swallowed. What was up with that dry throat? He wanted to be a pack leader almost as much as he wanted his alpha powers.

Or at least that's what he enjoyed telling himself.

Outside of internal-fantasyland, he'd rather let Margie lead the pack. It felt more secure that way. Not to mention the rush of knowing his mate had controlled a pack for years all alone.

Margie paced a line in front of the bleachers, answering questions and instructing those who wouldn't be fighting to help Allen in the infirmary. As he learned earlier in the day, the infirmary was the safest place on the ranch. Not even a pissed off werewolf could get through those locked doors.

He wanted to grab Margie and pitch her into the safety of an exam room.

Somehow he didn't think she would appreciate the gesture.

For better or for worse they were in this together. On the plus side, listening and watching how she handled her pack would teach him about how to do the same. He needed all the help he could get with pack leadership.

"Zane?"

Shit, instead of imagining himself running the pack, he should be paying attention to what went on around him. "I'm sorry. What was that?" *I'm a daydreaming fidiot.*

Margie's lips turned up as if she heard his inner thoughts. Which in his current state of mind, she very well might. "We were wondering how Sid normally attacks a pack. What's his MO?"

"He doesn't do it often. The last time he walked right up to the door, knocked and killed or captured everyone. No sneaking around for him."

"An egotist?"

"Yep. Overthrowing your pack might not be on his agenda. He wants Landa back and he wants me to return too. You'll have the element of surprise."

"Great. Here's what we're going to do."

Oh, hell no. No, no, no. Everything in him cringed as Margie explained how they were going to defeat Sid. His mate would play a leading role. A dangerous role. A role he should be playing. So why wasn't he front and center in the upcoming battle?

"Margie. With all due respect, I should be the one

to draw him out." Zane crossed his arms and gave her his best glare.

A raised eyebrow was her response to his tough stance. "Maybe. But I have a little secret that will surprise him. The plan goes as stated. Does anyone else have a problem with it?"

Judging by the headshakes and relative silence, no one agreed with him.

Shit. Until they mated, until their bodies joined as one, he had no right to tell her how to run her pack. No right to insist she not put herself into danger. No rights at all.

Damn shame he didn't have time to claim those rights.

A wave of humid air laden with the scent of impending rain greeted them as they left the gym, heading for the gravel drive he was told led to the main road. Margie motioned for her enforcers and Landa to follow, but Zane walked beside her, his baby blue slippers sliding through the grass.

"Your idea is insane," he growled.

Margie placed a hand on his arm. "No, it's not. Trust me."

Okay. He could do that. *Right?* Right. Trusting one's mate went without saying, but watching her put herself in harm's way was a whole other thing. He had this almost overwhelming urge to insist she not offer herself up for proverbial slaughter. To make a nuisance of himself until she did what he wanted. Zane pressed his lips together and clenched his fists.

Why the hell did he feel this way? This urge to protect, to kill, went way beyond how he had been told males felt when meeting their mate. This urge, this need was totally unlike him.

Your alpha powers are coming out. Margie's voice echoed through his head. *You're more aggressive. Or maybe you're just turning into one of those overprotective mates?* Humor tinged her voice.

How the fuck did you know what I'm thinking? Gravel crunched under his slippers as he came to a complete stop in the drive. *Did she read minds?*

Margie continued walking, forcing him to keep up. *Telepathy is a bit tricky as an alpha. It takes awhile to get used to. Watch that your emotions don't come to the forefront when you see Sid.*

What do you mean...a bit tricky?

Margie sighed. *You learned telepathy at puberty, right?*

Zane nodded.

You had to learn not to broadcast all your thoughts, how to put up a mental barrier so others didn't hear you. She paused.

Go on. He made a circle motion with his hand.

Well, alphas can communicate the same way with other alphas. Even if the alpha doesn't lead a pack. It's like a whole different channel. You have to learn to erect a whole different set of barriers around other alphas.

But not other pack members?

Right. Only alphas. That's how a pack leader knows which children will be alphas and which ones won't be. That and the aggressiveness most males show.

Abso-fucking-wonderful. Not only did he have to worry about his mate, his own life, the lives of his new pack and exactly how the fuck he would take out an evil sorcerer, but now he needed to worry that said sorcerer didn't read his mind while he attempted to kill the crazy bastard.

Where were his mental blocks when he needed them?

It's just like when you originally learned to block your thoughts. It's just a different channel. Find the channel and you'll be fine.

Thanks for the confidence.

Margie patted his arm. *No problem. That's what mates are for, right?*

What other alpha things can I expect?

That's a topic for a different day. I don't have enough time now to go through it all. But besides the thoughts, there shouldn't be anything else that will impede tonight's fight. Just guard your thoughts. Find that mental barrier and erect it.

Several hours, numb ass cheeks, and a full darkness later, his mental barriers were all in place, built and fortified. His mate sat cross-legged on the pine-needle strewn ground beside him, her enforcers spread out under the pines around the clearing. The gravel drive slithered like a snake into the trees, leading to the main entrance of the dude ranch, presumably where Sid would try to come in. It went against Sid's motto to sneak in and grab something, especially when said something sat under the trees opposite them. Landa had donned a black cap, which hid her blonde hair. Good thing too, since her hair glowed in the moonlight.

Zane stared at his hand, his human hand, twisting it back and forth through the shadows. Human. On the third day of the moon. For the first time in his life, he controlled the change, it didn't control him. He wanted to be in human form and surprise, surprise, he was.

"How do your enforcers stay human?"

Margie cocked an eyebrow, turning from where she stared at the lane as if she could summon Sid to their trap. "The alpha can cause a change in any of the pack members. If I want them to change into a wolf, poof, they're a wolf. If I want them to stay human, yep, they're human."

"Doesn't that drain you?"

"Nope. It's part of the powers that come with the label. You'll see." She waggled her eyebrows at him. "Do you think Sid's going to pass on tonight?"

"I don't know. I'm surprised he's waited this long."

"Well, he hasn't attacked the ranch house." She tilted her head to the side. "Nope. Everything's a little tense, but essentially all right."

As if their talking about Sid summoned him, the sound of heavy boots crunching on gravel whispered through the trees. By the amount of crunching, Zane guessed at least six enforcers walked behind Sid.

Okay, everyone. Get ready. Margie stood.

He would not lower himself to beg her to let him meet Sid first. Nope. She made a plan, and as much as he hated to admit it, the plan was a good one. Except for one small thing. He refused to hide in the woods while his female, his mate, marched up to the alpha who held his sister captive.

Not happening. Sid was about to breathe his last for terrorizing Zenia and Zane was more than happy to be the cause of that last inhale.

"Sorry, but I'm coming with you."

She opened her mouth, as if in protest, and then

shrugged. "If you must. But let me do the talking. This is my pack, after all."

Talking, he could handle. Letting her walk alone into the clearing to meet Sid, not an option. Zane walked a bit in front of Margie, not enough to where he led, but enough to where he could shield her body with his, if need be.

"Zane?" Sid's voice grated across his nerves, firing off a barely suppressed growl. The sound had no sooner died in his throat when Sid stepped out of the shadows, six enforcers forming a semi-circle around him. Thunder sounded in the distance, its faint rumblings muted by the trees.

"Hey, Sid."

"I thought you were dead. You've ... changed."

Yeah? Having one's engine turbocharged with alpha powers will do that to a person. "Have I?"

Sid stared at him until Zane felt his skin crawl. Standing motionless ranked up there as one of the hardest things he'd ever done.

"I'm Margie McLean, pack leader of London, Montana."

Sid smiled, his incisors gleaming in the moonlight. "I'm Sid and you have someone I want. I demand Landa back. She's had some rough times and must be kept under close supervision so she doesn't hurt herself or others."

"She seems fine to me."

Zane sensed Margie's enforcers creeping through the underbrush, surrounding Sid and his men. They were good, real good. Even with his heightened sense of hearing, he couldn't hear their steps, couldn't see them either. Sid's team of enforcers consisted of four males that would give their left nut to watch Sid die and two who were loyal. Not that being loyal scored them any brownie points.

He didn't take his eyes off Sid.

"She's not fine, not by a long shot. She's a good actress, but she needs to be returned to her own people."

"And you need six enforcers to return her?" Margie's hands were loose by her sides, but the pose didn't fool Zane, and he doubted it did Sid either. Tension rippled along her shoulders, pouring down her arms.

"Zane, hold her while I find out where Landa is." Sid took a step forward while Zane shoved Margie behind him. He heard her growl and didn't care.

"No. You're not hurting another female."

"What? How can you defy me?" Sid touched the torc encircling his neck. His eyes narrowed before popping wide. "How? Never mind. Your sister will pay for your insolent attitude."

"Like hell she will."

"Mark, take out Zane while I deal with the bitch." Sid touched the torc that lay around his neck, the torc that helped him control the actions of his enforcers.

Focus on Sid or focus on Mark? Or on Margie, who had slipped from behind him. *Shit.* Zane's gaze darted between the three of them, Mark taking the choice away. His best friend, one of the four who hated Sid, strode toward Zane, his steps stilted like a puppet on a string.

Zane, man, you have to take me down. Lurching like a drunk, Mark took two steps closer. *I can smell you're free of him. Use those new-fangled alpha powers to take me down before I'm forced to follow through on his kill order. I can only hold him off for a little while.*

Okaaaay. Instead of watching over his mate, or killing his former pack leader, he had to deal with the best-friend-under-the-influence-of-magical-torc syndrome. At least there was a cure for that.

Zane took a couple of steps forward, meeting Mark with his arm extended, fingers jabbing into Mark's throat. Mark gagged and bent over, reflex bringing his hands up to cover his throat. *Sorry, man.* Lacing his fingers together, Zane brought his palms down across the back of Mark's head, dropping his friend to the ground.

Thanks hissed through his mind as Mark slipped into unconsciousness.

Where was Margie? Zane started to turn as a bright flash lit up the clearing. He watched as a bolt of energy slammed into Margie, knocking her to the ground.

"NO!" The word roared out of his mouth, slamming through the clearing with the force of a tornado, ripping apart tree limbs in its path. He didn't think, nothing mattered but that his mate was injured, if not killed, and the one responsible would pay.

Before the echo of the sound stopped, he moved, running through the grass toward Sid who still stood with his hand raised, staring at Margie's prone body. His head turned at the sound of Zane's roar, eyes widening as Zane leapt, body changing, thickening until he became wolf mid-flight.

Sid managed to get one arm up before Zane landed on him, teeth shredding into skin, claws puncturing ... dirt? He looked up only to see Sid standing in front of him. What the fuck?

Sid laughed, his head thrown back. "It takes a lot more than that to harm me. The only reason you got your teeth in is you took me by surprise. What the hell happened to your torc?"

Sid held his arm close to his body, darkness staining his shirt and dripping onto the ground to vanish in the shadows. Zane growled.

"Don't answer me, then. It doesn't matter. You're dead and your pretty little sister will pay for it. Think on that in the afterlife."

Before Zane could move, a flash of light appeared in Sid's hand, only to be thrown his way. With a crash, it sank into his skin, under his skin, becoming part of him, as it charged through his system, fluttering his heart's rhythm. Pain exploded through his body, his muscles twitching in agony. He dropped to the ground, blackness beckoning, a comforting warmth, his friend and yet his enemy. The last sound he heard before succumbing to the darkness was all hell breaking loose around him.

Chapter Six

Margie looked at a prone Zane with a mixture of horror and anger, a twitch spasming her jaw. What the hell had Zane been thinking when he attacked Sid? The last few minutes of the good-plan-gone-bad ran through her mind as she remembered her shock at seeing Zane all furry. As she lay on the ground playing her part, being dead, she had heard him roar, the sound exploding through the clearing.

Her narrowed gaze had landed on Zane in wolf form as he jumped Sid. What the hell had he been thinking? He heard the plan, the plan that stated she would pretend to take the energy blast, pretend to be killed. Element of surprise and all. Once Sid thought her down for the count, she could use her own magic to take him out.

Yeah, her pack had been surprised at the "M" word and her use of it. Zane had been angry that she was putting herself in harm's way, but she hadn't thought he'd jump Sid. Had he forgotten about the plan?

Clearly.

What about everyone else? Had they forgotten the plan too? A glance around the clearing showed nothing but branches dancing in the wind. At least her enforcers' memories worked. She didn't see a one of them, but knew they hid in the shadows of the trees, waiting.

Sticking to the plan, unlike her mate. Five of Sid's enforcers stood along the inner perimeter of the trees, their gazes darting from where Sid stood, to Zane's prone form, to the dark shadows of creaking branches, obviously seeking her enforcers. Good luck there, hers were hidden but good. The sixth enforcer lay on the ground not far from her, a casualty of Zane's fists. One down, five to go.

Provided the plan wasn't clawed to hell. What had Zane been thinking?

When she had seen a streak of white light explode in her vision and realized it hit Zane, she thought a part of her had died. Just curled right up and expired.

Her jaw hurt from clenching it so hard, the muscle twitching in time to her heartbeat. Taking a deep breath, she relaxed her jaw. As if doing so opened a drain, the anger roiling through her system bled out, leaving behind a cacophony of other emotions. And surprise, surprise, horror won out. Margie's heart beat double-time, thumping like a drum behind her ribcage. Was he hurt? Was he even alive? She tried to swallow, but it stuck in her dry throat. To hell with the element of surprise, her mate was down and she couldn't lie around waiting for Sid to turn his back and not notice her.

But if she leapt up and ran to Zane like her legs were twitching to do, she'd put her enforcers and Landa in danger. Or more danger than they were already in. The plan was dashed to hell and back but she could still salvage some of it.

Taking a deep breath, Margie focused on calming herself. The forest sounds faded to background static as she concentrated on breathing, imagining a blank landscape before her eyes. No more clearing, no more mate, just her breath as it went into her lungs and out through her mouth.

In and out. In and out. Her breath expelled from her mouth in a rush, forming a small bubble of fog that hovered in front of her face. Another breath in and out and the fog expanded, circling around Sid's enforcers, blinding them, but allowing her pack to see clearly. Wasn't magic grand?

"What the fuck?"

"Where did that come from?"

She smelled their tension, their fear. Sid, who headed to where Landa hid in the shadows, paused, turning to stare at the fog surrounding his enforcers.

Not caring if Sid saw her, Margie rolled to her feet. Staying in a crouched position, she darted to Zane. Yells sounded from the fog, the roars of her enforcers, the whimpers of Sid's. When she reached Zane, she dropped to her knees, fingers seeking and finding his pulse. Unlike Mike, he didn't look like a crispy critter left in the sun to bake. If she hadn't seen him fall, she would have thought him asleep.

His pulse beat slow but strong under her fingers. Thank heaven Landa had removed Zane's torc, allowing his alpha powers to shine through. When Sid's blast smacked her down, she'd felt its strength, its power. But even if she hadn't thrown a shield of magic around herself, she would have survived it. Geared to take down a beta, the energy blast he threw would only knock out an alpha. Why Sid would toss a blast designed for a beta at an alpha, she didn't know. Hopefully it meant he wasn't as powerful as he liked to think.

"Zane?" she whispered, her mouth close to his ear. What would she do if Zane didn't make it? If her guess was wrong? "Zane, wake up!"

Nothing. She tried to swallow. At least he breathed.

A high-pitched scream cut through the night, followed by a deep rumbling bass of thunder. In a blink, Margie tracked the scream, following it until she saw Sid standing at the edge of the trees, one hand clamped around Landa's arm, dragging her out of a bush.

Another blink and she glanced to the sky. Despite the thunder, no clouds hung directly overhead, allowing stars to flit like diamonds on black velvet. Above the pines, black clouds perched like ebony cotton balls, blending into the dark sky. A third blink and she rolled to her feet, drawing energy into her palms until a ball of shimmering light danced on top of each one.

The SOB managed to knock out her mate, but he sure as hell wasn't taking off with her newest pack member. That happening was a no-go. Plus, he had some payback coming for taking out Zane. Not bothering with niceties, like, *hey Sid, you slimy bastard, I'm going to take you down*, she took two steps forward and lobbed a ball.

Landa's face lit up like a Christmas tree as the energy ball streaked toward Sid, slamming into his back. He stumbled into Landa, releasing his grip on the blonde's arm. Landa fell backward, landing on her butt as Margie darted toward Sid. Why wasn't he down? Sure, she didn't lob energy balls all the time—okay, hardly ever outside of the practice field—but that one should've knocked him down.

He recovered his balance, turning to glare at her as she ran toward him.

Despite telling herself not to, her breath caught at his appearance. White hair and a close trimmed beard gave him the look of a kind grandfather, if not Santa Claus himself. Although his flat gaze reminded her of portraits of killers flashed on the nightly news, dead and lifeless.

She threw her energy ball. He countered. His met hers with a blinding crash. Margie formed another ball and threw it, but Sid deflected it with a pop into a tree. *Whoosh!* The tree caught fire, flames licking toward the stars, the scent of burning pine filling the night. Sid laughed, a mirthless roar of air. Margie circled around him, heart hammering in her chest, muscles twitching the jitterbug. Her peripheral vision showed Zane moving—praise God—his feet inching forward, his body low to the ground.

Sid threw a ball and Margie dodged it, leaping toward the tree line, putting Sid's back to Zane as he turned to face her.

"Pesky fool. You're going to die tonight and your pack will belong to me." Another ball shot her way, this time nipping her in the leg as she dove behind a tree. Fiery shots of pain streaked up her leg as she dashed tears from her cheeks.

Dream on, jackass.

"No response? What, afraid of the big bad wolf?"

Maybe a bit, but she'd be roped and dragged before she admitted it.

She ducked another energy ball, peering from behind the thick trunk of a pine to see Zane converging on Sid. Muttering came from her left, Landa's lips apparently forming not-quite-soundless prayers. Margie picked up a rock and pitched it to her right. Sid turned toward the sound as the rock rattled against bark, thudding to the ground. She lobbed another energy blast right into his chest.

Score! Sid stumbled backward as Zane leapt forward, claws sinking into Sid's back. Canines flashed white as they attempted to bite into Sid's neck. One minute Zane latched onto Sid's back and the next he went flying, landing with a whimper. Margie jumped forward, flames burning in her hands.

Sid knelt on the ground, stretching one hand toward her. Even though he didn't touch her, she felt like he squeezed her throat, cutting off her air, his invisible grip crushing her windpipe. The flames died in her hands as she struggled against the invisible force. She couldn't move, couldn't fight it, couldn't draw in a breath. Dark dots danced across her vision as her ears caught waves of chanting coming from where she last saw Landa. Margie sank to her knees, her hands clasped against her throat, her eyes level with Sid's.

So this is what dying felt like.

She wasn't going down without a fight, dammit. As both hands clasped around her throat did nothing to reduce the choking pressure, she dropped one. Focusing her energy into her palm, she tried to summon a flame, but only a wisp of smoke danced and disappeared. She tried to move forward, tried to reach Sid, tried to stop him but his invisible grip around her throat held her immobile.

Fight him! Fight him!

Her mind gave the command, but her body refused to move. Dying. She was dying. Despite her wish, despite her will. Her gaze sought Zane, wanting one last glimpse of her mate before she died, before her life journeyed to a new existence. Where was he? The last thing she saw before darkness consumed her vision was Zane appearing in a rush of flying fur, soaring toward Sid.

****

Zane jumped at Sid, the force of his momentum shoving the sorcerer to the ground with an audible whoosh of breath. Margie toppled sideways, her hand still at her throat as she landed on the grass. He couldn't tell if she breathed or if Sid had killed her. A bone-shaking growl ripped from his throat as he swiped a paw across Sid's back. His claws seemed to slide off Sid's skin, shredding the shirt, but leaving the skin unmarred. What the fuck?

Sid scrabbled in a vain attempt to get out from under Zane. Not happening. Sid tried to kill his mate. Twice. Dying was too easy. Pain had its good points.

Before he slashed his claws against Sid again, Sid's torc began to glow like a red-hot poker. High-pitched humming vibrated from the torc, the same painful frequency as when Landa removed his own torc earlier in the day. Zane let loose with a howl before ducking his head between his legs and trying to stick his paws over his ears.

He heard Sid yelling, a string of no's running together so fast as to become its own ululating shriek. Right when Zane knew his eardrums would burst, the sound stopped like an electric guitar being unplugged.

"Noooooooo!"

Too busy trying to protect his ears from exploding, Zane rolled off Sid, allowing the alpha to scramble away. As Zane watched, Sid grabbed something out of the grass, muttering words over it. Whatever. Didn't matter what it was, those muttered words would be Sid's last.

Zane sprang forward, his claws ripping through the skin of Sid's back, blood wetting his paws. Sid screamed, a drawn out sound of pure terror as he dropped what he'd been holding. His torc. His source of power. Lying in the grass.

Biting into the soft skin of Sid's neck, Zane's teeth ripped and pulled, silencing Sid's screams forever.

Zane stood over his kill, staring at the man who had tortured his sister, denied him his powers, made his life hell and felt nothing. Nothing. Shouldn't he be excited? Shouldn't he feel relief? Shouldn't he get out of his own head and check on Margie?

As he raised his head, he heard movement to his right, a rustle of leaves, followed by scratching branches. Landa scrambled, half crawling, half walking to where Margie lay. Zane hustled to get to Margie first. She belonged to him. He needed to be the first one to check on her.

Sticking his muzzle against her neck, he sniffed. Blood pounded in the vein of her neck, pounding a rhythm that assured she lived. Air whooshed out his nose, a pent up breath he hadn't realized he held. Margie sucked in a wheezy gulp of air as Landa clutched her wrist, feeling for a pulse.

"She's alive! I thought she was dead."

I did too.

"Alpha!" Big G ran toward them, the rest of Margie's enforcers right behind him.

Zane turned, growling at the giant. In wolf form, instincts ruled and instincts told him to protect his mate, even against her own enforcers. For once Big G listened to him.

"Is she—" Eyes wide, he swallowed, unable to finish the sentence.

Calm down, Zane. Of course they're concerned, they aren't a threat. Margie is their alpha.

But the words didn't stop the growls from coming out of his throat.

Get a grip.

If he sucked in a breath, then he couldn't growl. Breathe in, exhale. Breathe in, exhale.

She's hurt. Pick her up and take her to Allen. And because it never hurt to be polite, he tacked on, *Please.*

Big G's eyes narrowed. Zane curled his lip. Big G dropped his gaze.

"Okay ... alpha."

Landa scrambled backward as Big G knelt beside a gasping Margie, lifting her easily into his arms. The giant's thoughts drifted back to Zane as his long strides headed toward the ranch house.

Your friends are unconscious at the edge of the trees. You might want to do something about that.

Okaaay. So he'd always have trouble with the giant, but at least he'd called him alpha. Even if it was spoken in the same tone as one would say "asshole," it was still a start. And as the working alpha on the scene, he needed to handle clean-up, as it was, instead of going with his mate like his heart urged him to do.

Landa, go with Big G. Make sure Margie is taken care of.

She nodded, running to catch up to the giant.

He raised his muzzle to one of the enforcers—was it Jace? *Show me where the others are. And you,* he nodded at another male, *dispose of the body. Just remember where you put it.*

"Yes, alpha."

No wonder Sid enjoyed being alpha, having everyone bow and scrape when they previously rolled their eyes would go to anyone's head. Working on not letting that happen would take some effort, but no way did he want to turn out like power-hungry Sid. He'd take a lesson from Margie on how to run a pack any day over how Sid had controlled his.

What should he do with his former band of enforcers? As he loped behind Jace he saw dark lumps upon the ground. Thunder rolled, closer than before, the wind joining in with its own accompaniment to the impending storm. He knew what he wanted to do with Sid's enforcers, but what would Margie do? This was her pack and territory they had invaded, not his. Not yet, anyway.

The strong coppery scent of blood thickened the air around the bodies as Zane drew closer.

Are they dead?

"Two of them. The others are just unconscious."

Which two?

Jace pointed out two lumps and Zane sniffed them. Yep, dead. One was a carbon copy of Sid, minus the magical abilities, while the other had been good, forced to follow orders he didn't agree with. What a waste.

They're dead.

Jace nodded. "They met up with Big G. He weren't too happy about Margie going down."

Zane knew the feeling. *Do you have a holding cell?*

"This ain't no prison."

Where do you put lawbreakers?

"That's what prisons is for."

I mean, where do you put pack members who don't follow the rules?

The enforcers glanced at each other, then at him, four identical confused looks.

Okay. Do you have a locked shed or something to put them in? Something they can't break out of and isn't close to the pack?

"The tack shed. We keep it locked so the humans can't get in."

Good. Take the ones that are alive to the shed. Make sure there isn't anything in there they can use to break out. And take their torcs off.

"Why their torcs?"

I'll explain later. And take the one I knocked out to the infirmary. He won't give you trouble.

"You sure about that?"

I know for a fact the locked doors down there are secure. He won't hurt anyone. And you, he pointed to a thick-set blond, *bury these two. In separate graves. Mark them so we can find them again.*

"Right on it, alpha."

He watched Margie's enforcers carry out his orders, watched as they lifted Sid's enforcers into a fireman's hold. Zane wanted nothing more than to run back to the ranch house, run down the infirmary stairs, and ensure Margie lived. But being an alpha, a good alpha, involved being a reliable leader, which meant he walked with the enforcers until they got to the tack shed.

After ensuring anything that could be used as a weapon was removed and the enforcers had no questions, he walked to the back door of the ranch house, intending to enter.

Which was a little hard to do with paws instead of hands. Change and walk to the infirmary in his birthday suit, or sit outside waiting for someone to help him? No choice at all.

Summoning his inner human, he forced the fur into hiding, exchanging wolf for human flesh. Sparks, like charged electrodes on his muscles, spread through his body, growing stronger in intensity as the change progressed.

Bones shortened, human flesh surrounded muscles, fur disappeared into body hair. Amazing. And he did it while the moon was still full. Hidden behind storm clouds, but still full. Even if he did stand buck naked in front of a ranch house full of pack members he'd just met tonight. Nope. No problem with the ass flash. For the second time in his life, he changed shape of his own free will. And that meant something.

Was that pull in his side normal when he changed of his own free will? He looked at the ache, surprised to see his gunshot wound open and trickling blood. Looked like an adrenaline rush masked pain. Good thing he was heading toward the infirmary.

Zane twisted the knob and entered into the large den, located at the back of the ranch house. He grabbed a leather pillow off the couch with "Cowboys Do It Best" written in large red letters, stuck it in front of his privates and walked down the hall, searching for the door to the infirmary.

Which door was it? They all looked the same. Wood paneling occasionally interspersed with a brass doorknob.

Wait. That one looked familiar. He paused,

drawing in a deep breath, scenting Margie behind the frame. A keypad nestled against the wood paneling, a red light at the top of it blinking a warning. Yep. That was the correct one. Right when he reached for the knob, the door flew open, banging him in the nose with a bone-crunching thud. Zane dropped the pillow as he grabbed his throbbing nose *Shit, that hurt.*

"Oh my gosh! I'm so sorry. Zane! Are you okay?" Margie's voice cracked, all hoarse and sandpapery. "Let me see." One hand touched the back of his wrist, soft and gentle, and he did as she asked, dropping his hands, tears streaking down his cheeks and dropping off his chin. A real masculine façade.

"I'm so sorry. At least it doesn't look broken, but let's let Allen take a look at it. Okay?"

"Fine. How are you?" A hundred hammers banged away in his nose. It might not be broken, but it sure hurt like hell. He dashed away the tears, not wanting anyone to think he cried over things like an almost-broken nose. Or seeing his mate alive and well.

Margie's eyes went wide and she glanced down his body, small tinges of red firing her cheeks. "I'm fine. My throat's a little sore. Looks like you dropped something." She bent, picking up the leather pillow. One side of her mouth escaped her control, turning up in a lopsided grin.

"Come on, cowboy. Let's get you some chaps so you can go riding."

Chapter Seven

Margie stood outside the door of the tack shed, taking deep breaths, listening to the rain pounding against the umbrella, dripping into puddles at her feet. The thing she hated most about her job was passing judgment on pack members. Luckily for her, her pack ran a step up from flawless, which meant this judgment passing she was about to do was her first. Glancing at Zane, who held the umbrella, she smiled. He stood by her. He would support her, from now until they died. Her mate.

Dressed in another pair of baby blue scrubs with little blue hospital slippers stained with mud on his feet, he nonetheless oozed masculine strength. Despite the situation, she felt warmth flow to her core.

Damn mating hormones.

Despite the hormones, not because of them, she wanted Zane with a passion she never thought she'd have for anyone. And he felt the same way about her. Tonight they would join their bodies and souls for eternity, forming a bond that would never die.

Right after they took care of passing judgment on Sid's enforcers.

Zane put a hand on her shoulder, nodding once. Thankfully Sid's energy blast did not cause permanent injuries to her mate. Under the scrubs, scratches marred his skin, overlaying bruises, and his gunshot wound—

what little remained of it—had reopened. At least that injury was small enough to need only a bandage, not another line of stitches. Another day or so and he'd be good as new.

You can't stand out here forever. Zane whispered in her mind.

I can try.

Putting off the inevitable made her look weak when she was anything but. Margie shut her eyes, dragged breath into her lungs through her tortured throat, shook her shoulders and exhaled. She nodded to Jace to open the door.

Big G and Jace walked in first carrying lanterns, shook off droplets of water, and stood on either side of the door, two guardians allowing Margie and Zane to walk between them. Bill and Ron, two of her enforcers, stood outside in the rain. Sid's enforcers huddled along the back wall, eyes blinking in the sudden light.

"I'm Margie McLean, the pack leader of London." Her voice cracked and she cleared it. Not like it helped. "I regret to inform you that you will be tried for threatening my pack and the attempted kidnapping of one of my pack members. How do you plead?"

Their pleas should be interesting. After listening to Zane's suggestion and the elders, she knew what to do. Provided they answered her correctly.

One of the three crawled forward, sitting back on his knees when he reached her, tilting his head to the side to offer her his neck. "I am guilty, but only because I was forced to do Sid's bidding. That does not excuse my actions. Do with me as you will. But if you would grant me a final request, please tell me why Zane is standing there."

"Zane is my mate. He stands with me. This is his pack too."

Three heads snapped toward Zane, identical wide-eyed looks of shock written across their faces.

"Any other pleas?"

Their gazes shot back to hers before dropping like good little submissives. Although calling what should be three alphas submissive seemed an oxymoron. Rather like a vegetarian werewolf.

Zane only told her one of the enforcers appeared to agree with Sid, while the others hated him. And then he refused to tell her which was which, wanting her to have an unbiased opinion on the matter. She assumed Mark was one of the good guys, seeing how he occupied his own locked infirmary room instead of being thrown in the tack shed, but she had yet to speak to him. Looking into dirty, stunned faces, she had trouble deciding which of the three took Sid's side.

A second enforcer went with the crawl and throat-offer routine, leaving one enforcer pressed against the back wall. His eyes narrowed on her, his gaze dropping as he walked to where she stood, stopping behind the kneeling enforcers.

"I'm not groveling like they are. I agree I'm guilty of what you accuse us of, but I'm not asking forgiveness. I did what I had to do, and I have no regrets. And if that means that you and Zane are going to kill me, then so be it. But I'm not apologizing."

She'd be willing to bet good money this one was the one who followed Sid out of his heart, not because he had to. The way he met her gaze, the tension coursing through his body, and his hands clenching and releasing, gave clues he would resist death to the very end.

"Do you know how to weave magic? How to bend it to your will?"

"Are you fucking nuts? No offense."

So much for the earlier submissive eye drop. This guy was about as submissive as an eighteen-wheeler going downhill in an ice storm.

"I take it that's a no?"

"Damn straight that's a no. No fucking way would I ever learn magic."

"Good deal. Go stand against the wall."

He backed up, his gaze never leaving hers. A worthy adversary.

Is he the one? She asked Zane.

Does what we discussed with the elders still stand?

Yes.

You're right. He's the one. I don't smell a lie on him, but that doesn't mean he's telling the truth.

And the others? Do you smell a lie on them?

Zane sniffed the air. *Nope. They're telling the truth. They're good males.*

"Bill, Ron, escort these two away from here." Margie gestured to the two at her feet. Water dripped off their hats as Bill and Ron led them away to her office to wait for their punishments.

"I'm afraid I didn't get your name?" Margie took a step closer to the remaining enforcer.

"Christopher Maas."

"Okay, Christopher."

"It's Chris."

"Chris then. Your punishment is banishment. You will leave tomorrow morning and will not return. If we ever meet and you cross me again, I will kill you."

Margie held out her hand, forming a small ball of fire that cast flickering shadows on the wooden walls of the shed. Chris's eyes popped wide as he tried to take a step backward, only to hit the wall. "Don't underestimate me. Don't see your expulsion as my weakness. Do you understand?"

His tongue darted out, licking his lips as he nodded. "I understand, alpha." His gaze dropped to the floor.

Margie closed her fist, extinguishing the flame. "Good. My enforcers will bring you a cot, food and drink. It's quite the storm out there, but it should be dry in here. Do you need your injuries tended to?"

"No. I'm fine."

"Then we'll leave you."

Zane stepped out the door first, popping open the umbrella for her. What a gent.

"Big G, Jace. I want a guard on the door until he's released tomorrow. Rotate shifts of two hours each."

"Understood. Have a good evening, Margie. And you," Big G pointed a tattooed finger at Zane, "take care of her."

"You know I will."

Talk about protective. Until Zane showed up, she never realized how much like a momma bear Big G acted. It gave an alpha female the warm fuzzies, it did.

But not anywhere close to the warm fuzzies Zane gave her. Who was she kidding? What she felt around Zane was nothing like what she felt at Big G's words. Nope. Zane warmed her from the inside out, heated her core to boiling and made her want to throw him down in the mud and sex him up until they both fell over exhausted.

One round of sweaty, mind-blowing sex coming up.

Right after they informed Mark and the other two enforcers of their punishments.

How fast could she walk to her office? And the answer? Pretty darn fast. Mud splashed on her jeans, covering her boots. Sideways blowing rain splattered against her raincoat, drenching her legs through the denim. So much for the umbrella. It blew inside out, a skeleton of metal ribs and cloth wings. Right as a crash of thunder sounded, they made it to the back porch of the ranch house. Zane dropped the broken umbrella on the porch.

Once inside, Margie stripped off her raincoat and hat, hanging them on the coat tree by the door. Office, more judging, and then for dessert, what she knew would be the best part of the meal—sex with Zane. Her boots clicked a frantic beat against the wood floor, followed by Zane's blue muddy slippers squishing out a melody.

Bill and Ron stood outside her office, the door open. The two former enforcers sat in leather chairs in front of her desk, talking in hushed tones. White stuffing stuck up in globs from the back of the left chair. What would they think of her housekeeping staff? She gave herself a mental shake. Why did she care? She was here to judge them for attacking her pack, not take their opinions on interior decorating.

All whispering stopped the minute she walked through the door, drying up like a stream in a desert.

"I'm afraid I didn't catch your names?" When would her voice stop sounding like a choking frog?

"Paul."

"John."

"Paul and John. As your punishment for attacking my pack, you will be indebted to us. Because you were forced to follow Sid, your lives are spared. For a period of two months, you will be our servants, the lowest members in the pack. At the end of that time, you will be allowed to join our pack if you want. Do you understand?"

Two identical bobbles marked her words.

"Good. What is your decision?"

The nodding twin bobbles glanced to each other, then back to her. Wasn't she polite not to eavesdrop on their silent conversation?

"We'll stay."

"Good choice. Bill and Ron will escort you to your rooms in the infirmary where you'll be under lock and key."

A couple of minutes later she and Zane stood alone in the office. Alone. Together. A predatory smile lit his face as he backed to the door and shut it, the lock sliding home with a resounding thud. So much for talking to Mark about his judgment. Not like she was complaining.

She grew wet as Zane stalked toward her, a wolf on the hunt for his prey.

"It's just us. No going back." His voice, deep and rough around the edges, caressed all the nerve endings in her body.

"I know. You ready?"

"Babe, I was born ready."

Margie shook her head. "That's just wrong."

He grinned as he pulled the scrub top over his head, dropping it on the floor. Muscles rippled with the movement, the bunching of his biceps enticing her. Springy dark curls peppered his chest, leading in a line over a sexy six-pack and disappearing below his scrub bottoms. Talk about being built. And all that strength and power was heading her way. Did she actually lick her lips like a starving dog?

"Do you like what you see?" Zane's dark hair framed his face as he took another step closer, untying the string that held the scrub pants around his waist.

"I'm enjoying the view. What can I say?" Boy, that was the understatement of the month. She wanted him like dried earth wanted quenching rain. Now and hard.

"I say I'd like to enjoy the view too." His eyebrows waggled in a suggestive way.

Oh, yeah. She might want to hop onboard the undressed-and-ready-to-go-train before it left the station. And while it would only take the work of a moment to undress, she wanted to see the drawn out pleasure in Zane's eyes as she slowly slid her clothes off. Death by stripping. What a way to go.

Inch by inch she pulled her shirt up, watching his eyes as the cloth skimmed over the skin of her stomach, passed over her breasts. She yanked it over her head and dropped it on the floor. His gaze fastened on her chest, heating her nipples into hard points that throbbed for his touch. Running her hands from her waist up over her ribs, she cupped her breasts, pushing them up against the silk cups of her bra.

"Do you like what you see?"

Nice to know she wasn't the only one pulling the lip licking routine.

"Oh, yeah." He let the scrub bottoms drop to the ground and toed off his muddy slippers.

Wow. What a package. And yep, there she went with the lip licking again.

Zane stepped closer to her, one hand reaching out to touch her face. "You're beautiful, my little wolf."

His lips lowered to hers, firm and warm. Her hands wrapped around his neck, holding him against her. The hard length of him pressed against her lower stomach as his tongue tangled with hers.

The kiss consumed her, igniting a fire deep within her. Day-um, but the male could kiss. Even her toes curled inside her boots. And she was way overdressed for the occasion.

Good thing Zane was on top of that little problem. His fingers had the button unfastened and her zipper down before her hands even joined the jeans-removal party. She helped him push them over her hips, removing her panties with the same shove, all the while maintaining lip contact. The whole damn ranch could catch fire and she'd still want to kiss him, to feel the press of his lips against hers, the rush of having his tongue touch hers. No other male had ever made her feel this good, made sparks of fire fill her veins to overflowing.

Foreplay might be wonderful, but she wanted him in her now. Wanted to feel the rasp of his skin against hers as he thrust into her wet core, wanted his essence to fill her.

Bang, bang, bang. Margie started, her movement breaking apart their kiss. The door shook from the force of some idiot's fists, bouncing in its frame like hail on parched ground.

"Who is that?" Zane whispered, his lips closing on her ear with a movement that must be illegal it felt so good.

"Mmm. Who is what?"

Bang, bang, bang. Oh. That. The idiot at the door.

"What?" She snapped. And what do you know? Sexual frustration fixed a raspy voice.

"Um, you wanted dinner brought?"

Yeah, okay, but that was before she realized there were other much better things to do with their mouths than chew and swallow.

"Just leave it outside the door and don't disturb us again."

"Oh. I'm really sorry, alpha." Dishes rattled as a tray was placed on the floor. "I'll go now."

Killing the hapless wolf wasn't nice, not to mention it would leave the ranch without its cook, so she swallowed the impulse.

"Sorry about that."

"Let's hope they don't come back." Zane's hands ran up her sides, fingers fastening onto her bra strap. Using a flick and a twist, he popped the hooks free. Margie slid the straps down her arms, letting the bra drop to the floor.

Now that was more like it. Flesh against flesh.

She lifted her lips for his kiss while his hands stroked from her back to her breasts, thumbs flicking over her nipples. Her hands moved across his stomach, brushing against his shaft, which jerked at the contact. Holding the thick width, she circled the plum shaped head with a finger, swallowing Zane's moan in her mouth. He took a step forward, clearly trying to head them in the direction of her desk. Being on board with that plan, she took a step back, or tried to. Her feet, still encased in boots covered with a layer of muddy jeans, stayed put. Zane's arm grabbed her, but the fall cost her the touch of his lips.

"It helps to walk when you don't have jeans stuck around your ankles." She gestured to her feet.

"You think?" He squatted, yanking off her boots, stripping her jeans and panties from around her ankles.

"Much better." Margie took a couple of steps backward, hopping onto the desk. "Come here." Two fingers beckoned him forward.

Wasting no time, he stalked toward her, taking her lips in a kiss as she wrapped her legs around his waist, the warmth from his skin sinking into the sensitive skin of her inner thighs. Shoving what little covered her desk out of the way, he tilted her back so she lay on the desk, his thick length touching her entrance.

She wanted this, wanted him. The selfish part of her that wanted to keep the pack to herself withered in the moment. Withered like a plant pulled up by the roots, leaving an empty space that was filled in a snap by her mate, her lover.

As long as she had Zane, nothing else mattered.

Slowly he thrust against her, in, and a slow glide out, again and again, each stroke rasping against her sensitive channel, bonding them together, joining them as mates. When he was deeply seated inside her, filling her to capacity, he grinned, the smile brightening his face.

"You're mine. Forever. And I'm never letting you go."

"As if I'd let you."

His smile widened as he pulled out, her inner walls grasping him only to release as he thrust back in. She closed her eyes, lost to the emotions coursing through her body. Lost to feelings of rightness, of oneness, that built into a mountain, a precipice she once found dangerous, but now wanted to rush toward, to hurtle herself off of, knowing Zane was there to catch her. Knowing Zane would always be there to catch her. Why had she feared having a mate? Why, when it seemed the best thing ever to happen to her?

No wonder the elders thought she needed her head examined.

Pressure built deep inside with each stroke, with each thrust in and out, over and over, until she didn't know where he ended and she began, until she cried out her release as the biggest orgasm of her life slammed through her. Zane kept thrusting and then he stiffened as he hollered his own release.

Margie saw the flash of his incisors seconds before he bit into the skin of her shoulder, a physical brand of their mating, the mark that would show she belonged to another. Removing his teeth, he lapped at the bite, sealing the wound. His lips brushed hers, a gentle touch of a bared soul. She touched his cheek with her palm.

"Day-um, Zane. I'll repeat that any time you want."

He chuckled as he pulled out of her, reaching for the box of tissues. He pulled a couple of tissues out and patted her between the legs. "That's good because I'm thinking the same thing."

Moving. She needed to be moving. Doing something besides lying in a satiated mass on top of her desk. With an effort she pushed herself up to her elbows, watching a nice flash of Zane's ass as he bent over to pick up his scrub bottoms.

"Maybe we should grab dinner and head to my

bedroom."

Zane yanked the pants on, blocking her view of his ass. Damn. "Where's your room?"

"It's in another building. Right next door." She glanced out the window. Did she actually have sex with the lights on and the blinds open? Good thing the rain kept most of her pack inside. Although the storm had died down to a drizzle.

"Sounds good. You might need to get dressed."

True. Easier said than done. But she managed. Did a half-assed job of it, but then, the clothes were coming off soon so runway-fashionable wasn't necessary. Zane already had the door open and the tray picked up by the time she pulled on her boots.

He turned to her, nose wrinkling. "There's a whole plate of grains and veggies on here and the meat is sized for one. Maybe we need to stop by the kitchen?"

Were her cheeks heating? Must be the post-sex flush. "I'm a vegetarian."

Zane barked out a laugh before he looked at her face. "Seriously?"

"Yep. You got a problem with that?" She crossed her arms.

His eyes popped wide, brows shaking hands with his hairline. "Nope. Just an odd choice. Whatever makes you happy, little mate. Wait. You don't expect me to do the same, do you?" Now his eyes widened for a whole different reason. Pure horror.

"Of course not. It's just something I do while human. I've been a vegetarian for years. No problems." Unless you considered salivating while looking at the sirloin on his plate a problem.

"There's a lot about you I'm going to have to

learn."

"Likewise."

He followed her down the hall and outside, carrying the dinner tray. Margie picked up an umbrella that hadn't turned inside out and popped it open. Holding it over Zane and dinner, she headed toward her cabin.

Zane made a face as his foot landed in a puddle. "We'll need to leave before they let Chris go. That way we can make it to my pack before he does. Provided he even returns."

"Are you nervous about going back?"

"Why should I be?"

She glanced over at him as he walked beside her and raised a brow.

"No. Not much. Zenia will be free and that's what I wanted. Not everyone will come back here, but enough will."

"We'll lead them together. You'll do fine. You got Big G to carry me to the infirmary."

Zane snorted. "He carried you because he wanted to, not because of anything I said. You're right. They'll accept me. But you're the real pack leader. They're used to you. You do a good job of it too. I can only hope to do as well."

"You'll do fine. Here we are." She opened the door to her—*their*—place, flipped on the light and let him walk in first.

Into her life, into her heart, into her pack. He was her mate, the one thing she never wanted, but now that she had him, she couldn't imagine life without him. Zane set the tray on the coffee table and walked back to her. The bruises from where his nose got in the way of her opening the door were already starting to fade. Talk about a fast healer.

"I'm so glad I found you." He bent to kiss her lips, reaching around her to slam the door shut.

She broke the kiss, placing her palms on his cheeks. "I'm glad I found you."

His lips touched hers and she was lost in the sense of peace that surrounded them. Her wolf mate. Forever

A word about the author...

By day, Karilyn works in the research department of an oncology clinic. By night, she tells the stories of her imaginary friends. Karilyn and her most wonderful, ever-patient husband share their home in the great state of Texas with two partially psycho dogs and a handful of colorful fish.

Karilyn loves to hear from readers and can be reached at <u>karilyn@karilynbentley.com</u>.